Wesley Yorstead Goes Outside

Wesley Yorstead Goes Outside

STEPHANIE HARPER

Writing Brave Press
1940 Palmer Ave. #1032
Larchmont, NY 10538
www.writingbravepress.com

Cover and Interior Design: Danny Meoño
Author Photos: Kyle Colby

Library of Congress Cataloging-in-Publication Data available.
ISBN 978-1-7375639-9-0 (paperback)
ISBN 979-8-9873704-0-7 (ebook)

Second Edition

In memory of Don Harper

Inside

Inside my apartment, I have everything I need. For a single inhabitant, it's more than sufficient, with a bedroom large enough for a queen bed, a spacious bathroom, and an open living space with a full kitchen. It has several windows and a door. People tell me the building is in a prime location, given that it's in the heart of the Mile High City. They tell me this is important. It's not a terrible city. I'm certain there are worse. I remember a field trip I took in grade school. I stood in awe on the steps of the State Capitol, with a round marker set into the marble, showing the exact elevation of 5,280 feet. It's how Denver earned its nickname. A strange sense of accomplishment overwhelmed me as I planted myself on that stairway, above so much of the world.

I haven't been to that bronze domed building in years. The stainless steel supports have eroded under decades of weathering and the uppermost portions have begun to crumble in structural decay. I haven't seen this myself. I haven't seen a lot of things. My apartment is on the third floor of an old brick building and if I look out the large window along the east wall of my living room, I see a park—a fragment of grass and trees imprisoned by towering condos on all sides. Concrete pathways weave through the area, with a bridge over the river. When the weather permits, these walkways convey people on bicycles, couples with clasped hands and disposable coffee cups, and lone women walking small dogs on florescent leashes. If I look farther I can see the Denver skyline hovering over brick buildings in the distance, glowing yellow-green against the night sky.

If I look.

I never open the window in my living room. I did once, the first year I moved. I'd begun to spend more time inside by then, aware that when I went anywhere, I'd become overwhelmed by the utter unpredictability of people and places. Anything could happen out there. This expectancy that something would happen tightened down in the center of my chest and made it harder and harder to endure any kind of new situation. Still, I had occasional moments when I longed to participate in some small way. And in a quiet instance of contemplation, I entertained the notion that if I opened my window for some fresh air, the sounds of the city, even a breeze, might ease the cabin fever. But the Platte River has always been rank with human garbage and the swampy aroma of moss and mildew, the noise of rowdy people traversing the sidewalk below grated on my nerves. I haven't opened my window since. That was five and a half years ago, six months to the day before the last time I left my apartment, the day I realized I'd never leave again. October 27, 2004.

I have everything I need inside.

Chapter 1

It's mid-morning on a Sunday in mid-September and the persistent knock at the door can only mean one thing: Angel's arrived with my groceries. Angel works for Lafferty's Neighborhood Market, a small place run by a boisterous man of Irish descent. The store has existed for four generations, since the original proprietors came over from the Emerald Isle. The original is in Manhattan. The current Mr. Lafferty's parents brought a satellite store to Denver, or so it says on the website. I've never met the man in person, but the sturdiness of his voice suggests he hasn't missed too many pints of Guinness over the years. What's important is that he's willing to send a delivery every week, and he doesn't ask a lot of questions. This makes his service indispensable.

Angel's the stereotypical grocery boy. He makes his deliveries in uniform black slacks and white button-down. He's got slicked back hair and a gold chain around his neck. If I were to sketch him, he'd sport oversized jeans that hung so low he'd have to waddle. Maybe that's unfair. He's been delivering my groceries for a while now, and he seems like a decent kid — always polite. He's quiet and unassuming and he gets in and out as fast as he can, which I appreciate because it means I don't have to struggle to converse with him. He comes in and puts my brown paper sacks on the stainless steel counter in the kitchen, then stands silent, looking at his feet. A month into our arrangement, he asked if there was anything he could do to help me. I sent him down to the mailbox to get my mail. Now, that's part of an unspoken agreement. I hand him my key and start to organize my groceries while he runs downstairs. I feel bad, making him run up and down, but he doesn't seem to mind and it's a federal offense to make a copy of a mail key. Not that I'd give him one anyway. He comes back and after I reopen the door, he hands me my mail, always with the key on top. Then, he waits for me to produce the magic checkbook and send him away with a little piece of paper, my signature scrawled across the bottom.

"How much?" I'll ask after I've checked that all my groceries are here. He recites the amount he's been given with an unobtrusive certainty and tosses me a sheepish grin. I return a small smile before ripping the check out and handing it to him. Then I'll open the locked box where I keep cash and slide a generous tip across the countertop. He'll take the money and disappear as inconspicuously as he entered, and I'll re-lock the doorknob, deadbolt, and chain behind him.

The buzzer rings again. This is unlike Angel, who might stand and wait all day if I chose not to answer. I don't bolt out of my chair. I'm in the middle of inking a preliminary sketch for my *To Kill a Mockingbird* project. It's jarring, being pulled away from my work like this. It reminds me where I really am. I place the cap back on my pen and blow across the fresh lines enough to ensure they don't go anywhere while I'm gone.

I take a few long strides across my front room, stretching as I go.

"I'm coming," I call out, though it's not entirely necessary. Where else would I be?

Before I answer, I pause to straighten my polo, check to make sure the collar is still turned down. I run my fingers through my light blond hair. It's easier for me to just trim the edges with a pair of scissors than to try and buzz it. Right now, it's a little long, and it falls in my eyes more often than I'd like. I smooth my gray slacks, careful not to mark them with any residual ink on my hands. I've always dressed professionally, even here in the apartment, when I'm the only one to see. It's one thing I can do for myself.

Angel pounds on the door. This is unfamiliar protocol, certainly not part of our well-oiled routine. I unlock the knob and remove the chain. Why is Angel behaving so aggressively? Perhaps he's running late with his deliveries. Maybe something's happened to make him upset or angry. I consider what I might say to him, how I might address his behavior, and I begin to feel that familiar pulling of taffy in my stomach at the implications of such a confrontation.

I have to be careful when I open the door. I have a peephole but someone, kids probably, covered it with black spray paint and I can't see through it. It was a surprising act of vandalism in my small building and mine was the only one. Despite daily messages to the superintendent, it hasn't been fixed. I think he neglects me on purpose. Perhaps he resents my persistence. I crack the door, expecting to see Angel with my sacks of groceries dangling from each hand like bunches of bananas.

A pale figure stands in the spot where Angel should be. A woman. She has natural red hair, curled to frame her round face, and she wears a yellow knit dress, ruffled in the front and hugged tight against her narrow hips. She's several inches shorter than my six-foot-one. She is not a grocery boy. My bags sit on the floor at her sandaled feet, her toes accented with black nail polish. This thin paper is all that separates the food I plan to ingest from the forest green carpet of the outside hallway, which is vacuumed perhaps twice a month. This means at any given time, upwards of two weeks' worth of my neighbors' filth has polluted the ground with dirt and bacteria. Not to mention that I know for a fact that there have been a couple of degenerates running around, filthy, with their can of spray paint. It'll take at least three harsh scrubbings to ensure the fruits and vegetables alone are safe to eat. I can't afford to get sick, given my situation. House calls are expensive.

"Finally." She bends over to retrieve the bags and unceremoniously pushes her way into my home. Her hair brushes my arm as she passes, so close I can smell the residual aroma of herbal shampoo. "Any longer and I was going to leave these in the hall." She places the bags on the counter in the kitchen and props herself against the edge. Her thin wrists contrast with her long, lean arms. They're delicate, contoured like flowing strokes on a canvas.

"Where's Angel?" I'm careful to stay on the other side of the island. She must be from Lafferty's. She carries bags with the name printed across in looping cursive, but my palms begin to sweat as I watch her, revolting against her uninvited presence.

"He speaks." She smiles but I don't look at her face for long. I settle on the length of her figure, the way her torso is the longest portion of her body, almost too long, because her legs are a little short. But she would be striking in a sketch. Not that I would do that. I've always preferred the freedom of creating figures in my head over the unpredictable intimacy of live models.

"Who are you?" I ask her. Mr. Lafferty hasn't notified me of any changes in our agreement. Now I have a stranger in my kitchen. She's intrusive and her dress is ridiculous. Angel is trustworthy, dependable, and monochromatically clad. This girl could be a thief, or some other impostor. Sure, she's arrived with the same bags my groceries come in each week, but that doesn't mean anything. The way her wrist bends as she pushes a stray strand of hair out of her eyes is deceptive in its tenuousness. My chest tightens. The safety of my apartment has been compromised. I squeeze my damp palms into fists.

"My name's Happy." She touches her long fingers to the center of her chest as she says this. I could keel over at the irony that this young woman, wearing an absurd manifestation of highlighter yellow, has a name like that. "Angel's grandma is sick again and he's taking some time off."

"Is she all right?" Angel's lived with his grandmother almost his entire life. She has severe asthma and it makes her prone to all sorts of complications.

"She has pneumonia. My dad sent me instead."

"Your father is Mr. Lafferty?" I cross my arms. If I'd thought about it, I could have surmised the familial connection. Her high eyebrows arched in my direction; she's a modern Maureen O'Hara. And, she appears to know a good deal about Angel. Still, you can never be too careful. "I should call him and verify."

"Go for it." She shrugs her shoulders and taps her fingers on the countertop behind her. I take my phone out of my pocket. I have his business card hung on the side of the refrigerator. It was tucked into my first delivery. On the back is a hand-written note, *"If you need anything, call."* I always do, to place my orders and complain about wilted produce. That's when the bacteria begins to grow. At this point, I know the number by heart, but I always check, just to make sure. I face her as I dial. She won't pocket anything while my back is turned. Someone picks up after a few rings.

"Lafferty's." The voice belongs to a man.

"Hello? Mr. Lafferty?"

"Just a minute." The voice disappears into the background noise of the store. Lafferty's deep baritone booms somewhere in proximity. I cross my free arm against my chest and furrow my eyebrows in the young woman's direction. She's unflinching, smug even, as she taps her fingers. Another moment passes and Mr. Lafferty picks up.

"This is Frank." He's a mouth breather and the sound of his dense inhale/exhale makes my skin crawl. I hold the phone away from my ear.

"This is Wesley Yorstead and —"

"Did you get your delivery?" He's always concise on the phone, though not always this abrupt. The store must be busy.

"I just wanted to discuss your delivery person. She says she's your daughter and—"

"Is there a problem with Happy?" He takes a deep breath. Someone shouts in the background.

"No. She's adequate." I make sure I look across the kitchen as I say this.

She lets out a solitary snort.

"She *is* your daughter, right?" I realize how foolish this sounds as soon as the words leave my mouth.

"Yeah, she is." Mr. Lafferty laughs on the other end. "Anything else?"

"Not today." I hear the click as he hangs up and I slide my phone back into my pocket. Now what am I supposed to say to her?

"Your total is $67.65." She rocks back and forth on her heels, pushing and pulling away from the counter like a buoy on the evening tide. Her constant motion is so unlike my own. I sit for hours at a time. That's why I wear the pedometer; my goal is 8,000 steps a day. That's also why I have a treadmill in my bedroom—I can take 6,000 steps just walking for an hour at a steady pace. I do it every morning when I wake up.

"You can sit." I turn and point behind me, toward the oval table. I don't want her to stay, but I'll try anything to keep her still. She's an alien in my house. This adds another load to the weight pressing down on my chest.

"I'm fine." She looks down at her square nails. Am I boring her?

"Suit yourself." I bend over the stainless steel island and press my pen to my checkbook. While I scribble, she turns a circle in my kitchen, like she just entered some kind of grand parlor.

There's a strange fascination in the glint in her eyes. The counter *is* spotless. It has to be. The CDC reports around 76 million cases of food-borne illnesses a year.

"Not much for decorating," she says.

"Guess not." I never saw the point of making the kitchen look like anything more than a clean space for preparing food. Besides, everything has its place.

I sign my name.

"Pretty fancy pen. You a lawyer?" She's referring to my Speedball Crow-Quill pen, a #107 Stiff Hawk nib, great for cross-hatching. Also suitable for my scrawling signature.

"Sure." I tear out the check. It's a knee-jerk response to her personal inquiry. Strangers always want you to explain yourself.

"I know you're an artist. I was just trying to make conversation." She leans down on the island against her elbows. My palms sweat like a glass of melting ice. She raps her fingernails against the steel and it sounds like the harsh pitter-patter of rain against aluminum siding.

"I understand." I nod like she's just delivered a piece of bad news. Maybe she has. The word "conversation" leaves a rotten taste in my mouth, like I've dotted my tongue with the wrong side of the pen and can still taste the ink. Besides, I don't appreciate the implication that she knows anything about me because that means I've been a topic of conversation down on the store or at her father's dinner table. The thought prickles my skin. Any kind of presence out there in the world can be a danger of one kind or another.

"Okay then." She pushes off the counter, her expression a

little crestfallen, and holds out her hand.

I pass her the check, careful our fingers don't touch. She turns for the door, just as I remember something.

"Wait." I reach into my back pocket for my billfold. "I have something for you."

She turns, re-crosses her arms over her chest. I head for my safety box of reserve cash. I keep the key in my wallet. That way, if I were robbed, they'd find the key to the cash instead of the cash itself. At least I've kept a sense of humor.

I take the small box to the island. My mother cashes checks for me about once a month when I need to restock. Happy's looking around the front room as though she's tracking a passing cloud. Her eyes settle on the framed print over my couch. It's a Kandinsky — *Composition 7*. Her head leans to the side as she takes it in. I can't see her face, discern what she thinks of it. You can learn a lot about a person by her taste in art. There's something intriguing in the extreme levels of abstraction — like a visual puzzle that needs solving. The artwork never gets tired, hanging there day after day. She's still staring — I can relate to that. It's easy to get lost in the shapes and color.

I clear my throat. "Happy's a different name." It feels like the right moment for an informal pleasantry.

"It's short for Harriet." She takes a step back and glances at me before her eyes return to the painting. It stands out against the white wall and olive couch below it, commands the attention of the room.

"I guess it's nice to meet you, Happy." The words spill out as they come — like the reluctant admission of a child after being asked if something really was as bad as he thought it might be. Not the best phrasing.

"I guess it's nice to meet you too, Wesley." She smiles and the lines around her face wrinkle in a natural way, as though smiling is something her face was created to do. But she said my name and I haven't given it to her. Another reminder that she knows something about me.

I force myself to breathe deeply and open the lockbox just enough to reach my hand in and not enough to show her the amount of cash inside. Being Mr. Lafferty's daughter doesn't earn her my automatic trust. For all I know, she could return tonight with some thuggish boyfriend to break down my door.

"Here." I hand her some singles. Our fingers touch. The shock of the contact makes me recoil with a sharp jerk, but she takes the cash without looking up and stuffs it in her shoulder bag. I return the box to the cupboard. When I stand, she's suspended in the middle of my living space, craning her neck toward my drafting table.

"So what kind of art do you make?" She takes a step toward the table.

"Graphic novels." I rock forward onto the balls of my feet. Frozen here in the entryway, I'm stuck not knowing whether the world is coming or going, inside or out. I don't mention any of the freelance illustration work I do when I'm between projects. Best to keep it simple.

"Comic books, huh?" She takes another step toward my drafting table and uncrosses her arms. "Do you have a favorite superhero?"

She's looking for Batman in my living room. I ignore her tone. People who haven't read graphic novels often sound this way when they try to talk about the genre.

"You don't approve?" As much as I want her to leave, long to return to my illustrations in peace, I goad her. Maybe I miss the opportunity to educate. I debated more than one high-minded art history professor during my undergraduate years. I even published a paper comparing graphic narrative to illuminated manuscripts of the Middle Ages. But I won't get into any of that now. Maybe I'm just curious about her interest in my work.

"I'm sorry." She reaches her hand toward me but doesn't touch me. "I'm sure you're really talented, but don't you think you comic guys should take an anatomy lesson?"

"How do you mean?" I ask. Mainstream comics have never been my area of interest, but I've studied enough to know where this is going.

"Impractically dressed women with beach ball breasts and waistlines missing ribs." I watch the way her mouth moves, like the hinge of her jaw is brand new — the smile perfectly instinctive.

The image of Catwoman pops into my head. Now's not the time to bring her up. "So?" I sit down in the swivel chair at my drafting table, the one I'd occupied for hours before she pounded on my door.

She sits on the sofa, crosses her pale legs. "Isn't it all about feeding the fantasy of horny fan boys?" She folds her hands in her lap and leans back against the couch, awaiting my rebuttal.

I can't say I wholly disagree with her. But she's talking about a particular cross-section. I should lend her Spiegelman or

Satrapi. But that would be premature; one can't just give *Maus* to anybody. I shrug my shoulders. "It's a visual art medium. Of course some artists focus on their interpretation of the feminine ideal. What art movement doesn't?"

My eyes drift to the square, oriental style rug on the floor, then over to my bookshelf, and the television fastened to the wall in the corner. It's a slight space, and it gets even smaller with her in it. The confines of my apartment, something I often relish in, seem to press in on me when any bodies are added. Lucky for me, I don't have many guests to entertain. I rest my hand on the unfinished drawing of Boo Radley out on the drafting table. Right now, it's nothing more than the outline of a man with no distinguishing features—an image adrift between something and nothing. This lack of completeness makes my fingers twitch with an urge to pick up my pen and finish it.

"Hellenistic Greece, 19th century realism, any number of modern art movements." She counts each one off on her fingers. She has that smug look on her face again. Something about her feels rehearsed, as though she'd prepared for this conversation ahead of time. Her motivations here are a mystery to me. Still, as sinister as this uncertainty feels, I've always been a chump for a brainteaser.

I should end this argument before it has a chance to spread its wings and flap against the heat of the living room. The pen in my hand is as heavy as a brick. It cries out to be put to paper. The longer I talk to this woman, the longer my sketch sits on the drafting table, less than whole. I don't have time to get into an art history debate with the grocer's daughter. I pull at the collar of my polo. "I liked it better when you were just looking at your nails," I say.

The apartment is starting to feel like a sauna. I get up to adjust the thermostat in the hallway leading to my bedroom. I turn the temperature down by two degrees. I'll return it to 70 degrees—room temperature—after she leaves. I close my eyes, take another calming breath.

She watches, shifting so her legs are crossed in the opposite direction. This doesn't bode well. "What kind of comic—I mean, graphic novels, do you write?"

"Graphic versions of literary works." I teeter at the edge of the sofa. I could sit. She's at the other end. There would be a whole cushion's worth of space between us—but I don't know how she'll interpret this, so I stay standing.

"Like what? Can I see?"

"I—"

"Please?"

Her abrasiveness startles me. She doesn't know me, and I don't know her, but she wants to see what I do. It's intimate, the idea of watching her survey my work. I don't have to see the faces of random fans who pick up one of my books off a bookshelf or order a copy online. And yet, I think of *A Study in Scarlet.* How might she react to the black and white, the ultra-realism of the *Country of Saints* flashback, the allure of Lucy—a kind of Lauren Bacall? I want to watch her expression change as she cracks open the cover.

"I guess," I say. I walk to one of my bookshelves, pushed against the wall on the other side of the couch and pull off one of my volumes from the center shelf reserved for my own work. "This was my first project."

"Hmm…" She runs her fingers across the cover, a black and white inking with the profile of a suave figure in a dark alleyway, high contrast with the title in bold, red letters. "Sherlock Holmes."

"It is."

"So, you took the novel and turned it into a comic book?" She raises her eyebrows, drinking in the cover.

"It's a little more complicated." I'm more than copy artist. I read words and see worlds and try to recreate my visions. It's about honoring the original but also making something new. And, sometimes, it's about absconding, to finding a place where the fear just doesn't seem to matter—not as much. I clasp my hands in front of me, stand over her. She has my book, and I want to stay close in case she bends it.

"Did you draw it all yourself?" She flips through the glossy pages carefully, giving each a brief glance.

"I did the writing, drawing, and inking. My colorist, Rick, fills it in."

"Sounds involved."

"It's a process." I take the book from her. Her eyes widen in a moment of protest, but the lines of her face soften and she settles back against the couch.

"So how does it work, doing someone else's book?"

"For this one, I turned Sherlock Holmes into a film noir detective. The whole thing takes place in Holmes' head. It's very Chandler." I scan my bookshelf, running my fingers along the volumes, pushing in spines that stick out farther than the others. There's a small comfort in this evenness. "Here's another one…" I settle on one of my more popular pieces, a test to measure her appreciation.

"*Hamlet*?" She studies the picture of a sad looking silver-blond clad in black, standing before large Gothic style windows.

"That one's big with lazy students and theater people."

"You have good taste." She's found the large images in the back of the volume—concept pieces of the Renaissance style castle, stylistic close-ups of ornamental portals and Dutch gables. She turns the book sideways to look at them. Her eyes move back and forth as she scans each image with careful deliberation.

I'd researched the entire history of Danish architecture to create a realistic looking palace. It took me over a year to draw it. The waiting drove Rick crazy. But I needed to believe that someone could find my palace erect at a site of Danish historical significance, that it really existed and I could go to it someday in another life or as a different person. The detail was so precise that I visited the palace time and again, knew every pane of glass, without ever leaving my drafting table. I'm almost positive a real building could never feel like that.

"Thanks." I replace *Hamlet* on the shelf, careful to ensure the novel lines up with the others. Then, unsure of what to do, I return to the drafting table. She sits on the edge of the couch.

"What are you working on now?" She points to the array of materials behind me, including a pile of model sheets of completed characters, an open sketch pad, and several pens with a fresh bottle of ink.

"I've just been commissioned to do a version of *To Kill a Mockingbird.* I'm working on a sketch of Boo Radley."

"He's creepy. Can I look?" She hops to her feet before I have a chance to answer and peers over my shoulder.

Why'd I say that? Of all the characters I've drawn, I find him the most troubling. How do you draw a ghost? How do you give him skin, teeth, hair, when he's an apparition in the window of a child's imagination? I haven't even begun to sketch those final scenes yet. It's hard to picture him in the flesh. He can't be real, not truly, until I give him a face. People need to see him to know that he's more than an apparition.

"These are just preliminary drawings." I shuffle the papers to hide the sketch, aware of the hair rising on the back of my neck at the sensation of her body emitting heat so close to my own. "Can you sit back down?"

She leans in to try and get a look. I hug the papers to my chest and swivel the chair away from her. My heart pounds and I close my eyes, afraid I'm about to succumb to the panic I've been suppressing since she arrived. But she straightens and sits back on the couch. She bites her lip and interlocks her fingers just below her chin as though she's about to utter a penitent prayer.

"Do you want anything?" I say. Something about her gesture unnerves me, and I need to change direction. But this question is silly. What could she want? What could I give her anyway?

"I'm fine." She waves her hand as though she's swatting at a fly. Of course she doesn't want anything from me. "Do you ever draw your own stories?"

"No." I don't have any stories of my own. Besides, that's not the point. The sketches crinkle as I clutch them tighter to my chest. The tendons in my hand sting with the ache to get back to work. "Haven't gotten around to it."

"Busy social schedule?"

"Something like that." I set the drawings down and reach for my pen, spin it between my fingers. She's made it clear that she understands my situation. At least her chiding is easier to respond to than a direct question.

She pulls her cell phone out of her bag and looks at it. "I've got to get back." She rises, straightens her dress, pulling it tight so the bones of her hips jut against the fabric. "You should put those groceries away."

I'd forgotten. They're still in the kitchen, on the stainless steel countertop, waiting. I hope nothing's spoiled.

"Thanks." I follow her, watch her hike her bag up on her shoulder. I unlock the doorknob, deadbolt, and chain and hold the door open for her. She pauses in the doorway.

"Do you think I could borrow one of your books? I'd really like to read the *Hamlet* one."

"I don't know." I shuffle my feet. The thought of one of my books leaving my apartment, going somewhere I have no control over, makes my stomach twist.

"I promise I'll take good care of it. I'll return it the next time I bring your groceries."

"You'll be back?"

"I think so."

If she plans on returning, I guess I could let her read the one. I turn for the bookshelf. She moves to follow.

"Stay there." I don't want her to come back in, lest she decide to stay. I'm not sure I have the energy.

She remains in the doorway while I locate *Hamlet* on my shelf. I cross back to meet her. As I hand her the volume, she smiles. "Until next time."

I nod and she strides down the hall without another word. After relocking the chain, deadbolt, and doorknob behind her, I go to the kitchen to unpack my groceries. What have I done? I'll never see that book again.

Chapter 2

"If you knew it was an issue, why'd you lend it to her?"

It's Wednesday afternoon. Dr. Kidman's here for his weekly duty call. Every Wednesday, he leaves early from his campus sanctuary so he can stop by for our unconventional session on his way into the suburbs. He continues to come because he's known my parents, the civil rights lawyer and his wife, for decades. It's an obligation of friendship. I try to avoid those. His diligence over the past several years should feel encouraging, except that it means I have to talk to him once a week. It takes a great deal of forethought to consider what I might say ahead of time, plan answers to any number of his frequent inquiries. I run through a list of hypothetical questions, some more likely than others, because if he catches me off guard I might say something that could be damaging to one or the both of us. I'm exhausted before he even knocks on my door.

"I guess it's my vanity." I'm on the couch—the most appropriate spot for our interaction. The good doctor has positioned himself in my armchair, one leg crossed over the other. He looks at me over the thin rims of a pair of reading glasses resting at the tip of his nose. I suppose he's attempting a father-like aura, trying to appear more approachable to his students and study subjects. If I weren't so anxious, I'd tell him he looks like a less interesting version of John Lennon.

"Don't start that again, Wes." He massages his temples with the tips of his swollen fingers. This conversation isn't new. He's tired of it. He also knows it's his own fault. He planted the seed.

"What was it again?" I stretch my arms up over my head. It's been a long day at the drafting table, and my shoulders feel stiff. "Glib narcissism?" I offer the phrase like a faint memory, though we both know I recall the exact words like he carved them into my skin. I've had a lot of time to think about it since he said it during his visit two weeks ago. I shouldn't care so much; we're all narcissists. Still, the phrase left the Doctor's lips and somehow the words became a filleting knife. They cut through me, thread by thread, the more I think about them. We haven't added "narcissistic personality" to the list.

"Slip of the tongue." He looks out the window, readjusting himself in the chair. He knows he created this monster and his defensiveness is his remorse. Usually, he's more charitable.

"You did say it though." I cross my arms over my chest. I'm never comfortable on the couch or I'm never comfortable with the Doctor in my apartment. Even as long as I've known him, he's still an outsider here, and he could bring any number of pieces of that unpredictable world into my carefully coordinated space. He's a danger the second he walks in the door. I shift against the cushions and wait for his response.

"What would you like me to say?" He looks at me with a wilted expression. I don't have the answer to his question. I want him to extract the thought from my head, tell me why I can't let this go, give me a simple exercise to fix it. I want some peace of mind.

"You're the expert." I pinch the bridge of my nose, eyes closed. I can already feel the tendrils of unease tensing the muscles in my forehead.

"I thought we were talking about the woman who delivered your groceries."

"She's unimportant." I smack myself lightly on the side of the jaw with an open hand. It's an open dialogue with my nervous system, a way to refocus my attention, convince my body that the headache isn't necessary. The Doctor's seen me hit myself so many times before, he doesn't even flinch. That in and of itself should be an indication of what his presence does to me. What I hate most is how he always tries to change subjects, steer the conversation in the direction he wants to go. I won't let him control this. I open my eyes just long enough to see him nodding. If he were taking notes, he'd be scribbling something now. "I'm waiting," I say.

"Diagnostic criteria are not a checklist, Wesley and I don't want to play games with you."

"Humor me." I put my hands out, pleading.

He takes a deep breath and lets out a heavy sigh. "Do you react to criticism with rage, shame, and/or humiliation?"

"Doesn't everyone?" I swing my legs onto the couch, turning so I can lay my head on the armrest. The Kandinsky painting stares down at me from the wall. From this upside down angle, its shapes and figures are even less discernible. The strangeness of looking at something I'm familiar with in this alien way makes my heart race. I cover my face with my arm. I'm tired of watching the Doctor anyway.

"Do you take advantage of people for personal gain?"

I'm starting to remember how juvenile this was the last time. Everybody uses everybody. If I did take advantage of people in a truly heinous way, I'd never cop to it. I shake my head.

"Feelings of self-importance?"

I laugh.

He grows more frustrated with each unanswered question, but I don't dignify them with a response. After all, this is supposed to make me feel better about myself, remind me that I could be worse. "Do you exaggerate your talents and achievements for admiration and attention?" Yes, this is better. I'm not this unbearable. He sighs. This is the one he's been waiting to ask, and I've been waiting to answer. "Lack of empathy?"

"That's the one." I'm having déjà vu. This is what we were discussing the last time he called me a narcissist. During the conversation that started this, he was trying to tell me about his daughter's ballet recital. Sometimes my anxiety makes me forget to seem interested.

The Doctor takes off his glasses and leans forward to stare at me. I turn my head against the armrest of the couch—pressing the plushy texture to my cheek has a calming effect. He doesn't seem to have an answer.

"What's your diagnosis?" I ask.

"Wesley." He exhales my name in a drawn out sort of way, like a toilet that hasn't stopped running. We do this often. I try and force him into some kind of sardonic psychoanalysis, when that's not why he's here. He's not even a practicing shrink. He's a professor. He researches the biological, cognitive, and experiential differences in adult and juvenile depression and subsequent treatment implications—something I've heard him say enough times to recite it myself. He comes here because he cares about my family, about me. He can handle seeing me like this, when they can't. My anxieties only serve to amplify those of my mother's—a vicious cycle. My father can't stomach the idea that someone like me came from his DNA. This all gets worse with each passing year. Dr. Kidman's being here helps them cope. He lets them believe there may be hope for me. At the very least, he comes over with regularity so they don't have to. The rest of it is just a game—a way to distract ourselves from the fact that we both know he has to report his findings, my total lack of improvement, to my parents.

I hate the way he stares at me from behind his salt and pepper beard. And his glasses are outrageous. I get a restless tingle in my legs. My hand throbs with the absence of the pen I've been holding. I need to do something physical, something to ward off the feeling that my apartment might collapse in on itself, how it always feels when someone else invades. Perhaps I'll have a snack.

I get an apple out the fridge and take it to the sink. While this apple's been washed three times already, it's been in the refrigerator long enough to acquire a buildup of some kind.

Refrigerator salad drawers can contain upwards of 750 times the amount of bacteria considered safe. I spray the apple with

FiT and dry it with a paper towel. Then, I place the necessary instruments before me on the island, so I'm facing the Doctor. I press the edge of the sharp knife into the reddish yellow flesh and push. It slices with ease and the knife thwacks against the silicon cutting board. The apple falls into two halves.

The Doctor takes a pack of gum from the inside pocket of his jacket and pops a piece into his mouth. He neither turns nor asks what I'm doing. He understands. "Wesley, we've talked about this before."

This consists of severe social anxiety, panic disorder, agoraphobia, and an intense fear of illness and death manifested in a variety of obsessive tendencies. There are other buzz words. Trauma. Fear mechanism. Behavior modification. All things I'm acutely aware of as they run my life on a day to day basis, but can't quite grasp ahold of. So they float between us as shared language, one of us living the definition the other tries to explain.

"Forgive me, I'm neurotic," I say. I turn one of the halves over on the cutting board and place the knife against it once more. It splits as I press down. I remove the core, careful as the steel edge of the knife moves closer to my thumb. Once the other side is quartered, I scrape the inedible pieces into the garbage underneath the sink, plug the drain, and fill it with hot water. I always do my dishes right away. It's hazardous to leave them dirty.

The Doctor chews his gum loud enough that I can hear him from across the room. The sound forces my shoulders upward, as if I could plug my own ears. Gum is so unnecessary. "You shouldn't downplay the complexity of your situation, Wesley." It's difficult to dwell too much on what he's saying when the sound of his gum makes me feel like there's a shooting range in my living room. "And since you won't take anything they've prescribed..." Another buzz word: Zoloft. Everybody wants to put me on something. Doctors always do.

I tried antidepressants in college, but between the nausea and the increased restlessness and insomnia, I decided I was better off without them. I went to a few sessions with a counselor at the student center, thought that if the medicine didn't work, maybe talking to someone would. After two sessions, the counselor told me that the severity of my issues was beyond the scope of the student center's services. He gave me a piece of paper with the names of some local practices and told me I should make an appointment elsewhere. I never went back and I never called anyone else, in part because there were too many complications with scheduling and transportation, and in part because I thought what he was really telling me was that I just couldn't be helped. My feelings about the latter have only intensified over the years.

Steam rises from the sink. Doctor Kidman's presence naturally brings my thoughts to my parents, and something about the way the steam curls up from the stainless steel basin calls to mind a hike I took as a child to a natural pool near Pagosa Springs. It was one of those streamside springs, with a manmade edifice of stacked rock that separated the small soaking pond from the San Juan River. The pool was a unique treasure for my parents, no more than three feet deep, and just big enough for our family to fit. My mother, always fearful of the possibility of getting caught unprepared in an oncoming storm, found the clear blue sky perfectly to her liking. My father was elated to discover the spring empty, like the water had sprung forth from its crack in the solid rock just for us. It was an idyllic moment as my parents settled in, soaking their bodies in the warmth of the pool. I wouldn't join them. The stench of the sulfur burned my nostrils and the water was so inexplicably hot. It was like the boiling pots that banned me from the kitchen when my mother cooked. I might knock one over on myself. She was always terrified that some calamity might befall her only child. By that age, I'd learned from her example and started waiting for disasters too. This kept me standing on the banks, arms crossed in defiance, as my parents begged for me to join them. A lot of my childhood memories end like that.

I squirt the dish soap, turn off the faucet, and slide the utensils into the water. It has to be hot for this to work. My apartment doesn't have a dishwasher and while I can't bring the temperature of the water up to the 145 degrees that would guarantee a quick and certain death for the bacteria, I can make a solid effort. My hands are red. Is this how the spring would have felt that day?

The steadiness with which the Doctor chews his gum allows me to keep my back to him, because I know he's settled. When the intensity of his smacking increases, I glance over my shoulder, hands teetering on the surface of the dishwater. The awkward, sideways motion of his jaw is more bovine than human. The recliner creaks with the shifting of weight, and he gets up, comes to stand at the other side of the island. He'll talk to my back. He's safe here in the kitchen and if I can't see his mouth, maybe the noise he's making won't seem so disruptive, a constant reminder of his presence in my ears. I arch my back away from the sound.

"Look," he says and cracks a bubble like the troublemaker in the back of the room, snapping his pencil just as the teacher calls for silence. "You brought up this girl and—"

"Damn it!" I drop the cutting board and hot water splashes against my torso. My shirt soaks up the brunt of the water. My stomach is safe. I grab for a dish towel and blot at the mess.

Doctor Kidman raises his hands like he's talking someone off a ledge. "Don't get upset." The psychologist types like to pretend every crisis is a notable one. I think he enjoys the drama. "We'll talk about whatever you want."

"I'm tired of talking." All we ever do is talk. I have to change my shirt, but I can't leave him in the living room by himself. It's not that I don't trust him, but anything could happen while I'm back there. I can't trust the idea that something won't. I pick up the cutting board and return it to the sink, resume scrubbing. Then I look at the Doctor as I dry it with the towel. "What's wrong with me?"

This isn't the first time our conversation has settled here. Early on, he might stand by and watch as I struggled to leave. I used to try. Sometimes in front of the Doctor. Sometimes when I was alone, or at the coaxing of Rick or my parents. But I could never bring myself to take that first step across the threshold and out into the hall. It never mattered how much I wanted it, how much I thought I needed to do it. I couldn't. So I would cry or get angry. Bang my head against the wall. I'd beg the Doctor to fix me. But he never could. It wasn't his job. It was mine, and

I've never gotten further than trying. I don't even really do that anymore. What's the point? The Doctor was the first one to stop pushing, to understand what had happened to me long before the rest.

He sighs and places both hands on the edge of the island. His direct eye contact makes me antsy, but his body language tells me what he's about to say is too important for me to look away. "The words 'totally' and 'fucked up' come to mind, but that doesn't really get us anywhere."

This may be his most colorful answer to date.

"I appreciate your honesty." This is part of a whole collection of catchphrases—trite and simple—that I use sometimes. It makes it easier to relate to people, to say the predictable things, the things I think they want me to say. Besides, I don't have the energy to be more original right now. I return the cutting board back to the cabinet.

"Tell me about the grocery girl." He's still itching to talk about this. I wrench the knife out of the hot water, wrapping the metal handle in the dish towel so I can hold it. The heat against my fingertips straddles that border between scalding and invigorating.

"What's to tell?" I slide the knife back into the wooden block and unplug the drain. The water funnels out—anxious to be free of my sink. I run the towel along the edges of the counter, careful to remove any residual dishwater. Then, I wash my hands and dry them on a fresh dish towel. When the kitchen's restored, I move past the Doctor back into the living room, hoping to return him to a seated position. He's shorter than I am, but solid.

His broad chest and stocky build still reflects his high school wrestling career. I'm tall and bony. If I go too far, say something rude about his daughter again, he could lift me and throw me against the wall. Not that I think the Doctor would hurt me — just an involuntary flash of imagined violence. Still, I would hate for something to happen to the Kandinsky.

"What's wrong now?" The Doctor hasn't settled — he needs to sit down. Then again, maybe he needs to stretch his legs. He sits all day, I imagine, listening to depressed housewives and suicidal teens. Maybe he gets as restless as I do. That reminds me. I glance down at my pedometer. 7,563 steps — right on track.

I catch a whiff of dirty water — the drying mess on my shirt. My skin crawls against the dampness. I suck in my stomach, try to hold it away from the fabric. "Can you please sit?" I hate when I have to ask him these things; it reminds us both that I'm strange.

The Doctor nods as he takes a seat. He glances at his watch: a large silver piece with a round, black face and simple diamond accents. It's a nice watch, an Omega. The good Doctor paid a pretty penny to keep time with the world. I don't wear a watch. Besides, we're not on the clock and he's not getting paid. Why does he need to look?

"Why don't you want to talk about this young woman?" he asks.

I laugh out loud. He's really cracking the egg now, trying to manipulate me into self- reflection — a regular Sigmund Freud. Pretty soon he'll be trying to convince me she reminds me of my mother. "She's frustrating." She disrupted my space and she stole my book. I'll never see it again and it was my very first copy. The temperature of the room swells. I unbutton the top button of my shirt. "She's nosy."

"What did you talk about?"

"My work."

"That must've been nice." He glances at his watch again. Perhaps I'm keeping him from another ballet recital. I should remind him that he can leave anytime.

"I don't know. It was fine." I get up to adjust the thermostat, make the room feel right again.

"Could you be more specific?" This is his favorite question. He's said it so many times he doesn't realize he says it anymore. What is he getting at anyway? Do I like that she asked me? Do I enjoy talking about my work?

"I don't know what you want from me." Whatever he's suggesting, it has nothing to do with Happy. The only reason I brought her up in the first place was because I want my damn book back. I start to pace the floor, following the familiar track across the rug. He makes me nauseous.

"Hmm." He looks at his watch a third time.

"Am I keeping you?" He wants me to ask. He wants me to give him permission to go.

"Just dinner with the girls." He always refers to his family this way. With a second wife and two young daughters, I suppose this makes sense. I'll never have to worry about getting home within somebody else's timetable.

"We're done here," I say. I need to change my shirt anyway. I still smell the dirty water, even now that it's dried, and the uncleanliness makes the bile rise in the back of my throat. I taste the acid on my tongue.

"If you say so." He nods like he wants me to think he's sorry to be going, but I can see the spark of relief. I walk him to the door, unlocking it at a slow pace, feeling his stare as he watches my every move. A spy in my apartment. My parents rarely come and see for themselves—once every few months maybe. What will he say? Will he tell them about Happy? Does it matter if he does?

"Until next week," I tell him as he heads out the door. He's a part of the routine, after all.

"Yes. Next week." He smiles and for a brief second I'm almost sad to see his stupid glasses turn away. Maybe I should have tried harder. I could have answered his questions. We could have spoken just a little longer. He stalks down the hall, bobbing like Rocky Balboa before a big fight, pumped to get out of the solitude and back into the ring. It's better he's gone. If I don't change my shirt, I'm going to throw up.

Chapter 3

It's Friday and I've had to call for groceries a few days early because my peaches are moldy and I'm out of fruit. This won't do. Natural antioxidants protect the body against cell damage and fighting off disease is of the utmost importance. My delivery should arrive any minute and I can't sit still. I asked Mr. Lafferty if Angel would be returning. He gave me an emphatic "not yet." That was all he said on the matter. I imagine his replacement has been here once before. She still has my book and I want it back. What if she's bent the cover? I hate when people roll a soft sided novel in their hands. The cover never rests quite right after that. Books are flat for a reason. I'm pacing. I've sat down at my drafting table, ready to draw, about five times since I called in the order, but I just can't relax. It's probably added an additional 500 steps to my daily activity. I suppose that's not a bad thing, but my heart races. The vein throbs on the left side of my neck. I raise my arm to look at the armpits of my pale blue dress shirt. The fabric is damp with sweat. I'll have to change. There's a loud rap at the door.

"Who is it?" I ask, with the tips of my fingers pressed against the wood.

"Groceries." I can hear her lightness through the door. I undo the chain.

"Hello again." She smiles, my bags again on the floor at her feet. She has my book in the crook of one arm and a clear, glass vase of daisies in the other.

"Hello," I say. She's pulled her hair back in a tight ponytail, anchored at the crown of her head. The skin of her forehead is taut and her eyebrows appear even higher than the last time I saw her.

"Can you grab those?" She crooks her neck toward the grocery bags. Then, she passes me and sets the glass vase in the center of the kitchen island. I stand in the doorway. Could I manage to reach out and pull my groceries inside? I can't risk exposing myself in that way. Anybody could be out there in that hall. Just look what they did to my door. I squeeze my eyes shut, swallow back the nausea. I can't.

She returns and retrieves the bags. "Or not," she says as she brings them into the kitchen.

"What is that?" I speak only after I've re-locked the door. Then, I settle on the daisies—full, white petals with bright yellow centers. I've already written out the check with the total Mr. Lafferty gave me on the phone—a welcome variation in the purchasing process that sometimes occurs when orders are small and easy to calculate. The check waits on the corner of the island along with a cash tip. She grabs the stack, folding it in half with her slender fingers, and slides the wad into her back pocket. Not the safest place for all that money. I hope she isn't mugged on the way home.

"Those are called flowers," she says and begins to unload my groceries.

I make tight fists, watch her handle my food as though it's her own. My head starts to hurt, a sharp pain in my left temple. I'm probably allergic to the flowers. "What are they doing there?"

"I thought your kitchen could use a little color. Where do you want these?" She dangles the plastic bag of fresh peaches.

"What are you doing?" With my food. In my kitchen. In this apartment. I don't understand. I rip the peaches out of her grasp. "I can put my own groceries away." The array of food on the counter looks like a street market. I pause a moment, reach up and give myself a little tap on the side of my cheek, try to refocus the pain in my temple. I ignore the feeling her stare induces — like meat hooks digging into my stomach — and begin organizing everything in appropriate food groups.

She bites her lip. "I was just trying to help." The look reminds me of a well-intentioned babysitter I once had who thought the best way for me to get over my fear of the dark was to shut me in a closet. The teen bore a similar expression when my father lectured her, while my mother cradled me on her lap. My mother's arms shook as she held me.

"Don't," I say.

Happy wears a plain white t-shirt. It's a looser fit, and if she were an artist's model, it would be much harder to draw her curves today. In truth, I always hated that part of my studio courses. It was difficult for me to focus on my sketches with a live model. I hated the naked male models because penises have always made me uncomfortable, and the eyes of the women with shaved pubic regions always seemed to find me, no matter how hard I tried to hide behind my easel. I never enjoyed portraits anyway. Real people only remind me of my real life, and once I start thinking about that, I think about everything else, how I got here and how I'm never leaving, and then I just can't stop. None of that exists when I'm invested in recreating another person's story. No, I don't miss art school at all.

"Excuse me." I push past her and open the refrigerator door. The drinkables — like the fresh carton of soy milk — go on the top shelf. Then I have a fruit and vegetable shelf — fruits on the right and vegetables on the left. Below that is protein. Today, I have free range chicken breasts and wild caught Mahi Mahi. Any sauces or dressings go in the door, along with eggs and butter. The fresh bag of salad mix goes in the crisper drawer. I close the door and move to the freezer, adding a bag of frozen berries to the near empty space, alongside a few bags of vegetables in self-steaming microwave bags. There's also a container of vanilla flavored Rice Dream frozen dessert and a few ice packs. I don't eat dairy. It's not sanitary. Studies have suggested that the hormones in cow's milk may cause cancer.

"That's quite a system." She's watching me as if she's pressed me under a microscope.

"I like to be organized." I know what it looks like. She probably thinks I'm obsessive compulsive. I'm not really. It's just that arranging my food this way makes it easier to ensure there's no cross-contamination. And, it helps me visualize the different food groups — a balanced diet is vital to ensure the body functions properly. I begin to put the dry goods away, having divided them into snack foods, dinner supplements, and breakfast items. The fresh loaf of bread goes in the bread box between the microwave and the toaster. She leans against the island. The flowers are still there. "You shouldn't have brought those."

"Too girly?" She raises her eyebrows.

"I don't have things like that in my apartment." It's hard to make her understand why this bothers me as much as it does, but I look at the vase and it's like a tiny colony of ants crawl across my face. The petals will die and fall dry and brittle onto the island. I'll have to clean up the mess. And the stagnant water in the vase could be a hotbed of bacteria.

"There's a first time for everything, right? They brighten things up." She reaches out and adjusts the vase, centering it.

"Okay," I say. I can always figure out what to do with them after she leaves.

She laughs.

I put the empty grocery bags under my sink, hoping she doesn't catch the small flush in my cheeks. It's getting hot in the apartment again.

"Here's your book." She slides it toward me. I inspect it for damage, flipping through the pages, looking for stains or smudges. Nothing appears ripped or bent.

"Thank you," I say, returning it to its place on my bookshelf. I should ask her something, what she thought, but this might seem vain and I might not like the answer. I don't say anything, let my hand linger on the bookshelf, avoid turning around.

"Thank *you*." She follows me and sits down on the couch, the same place she sat the last time she was here. "You're very talented."

"Glad you liked it." I take a deep breath and turn to face her. It's true. I did want her to enjoy it. Rick goes to conventions sometimes, interacts with our fans on social media. Sometimes he brings me the occasional review. But, it's different seeing someone react in person. I sit down at the dining room table, turning my chair to face her.

"How did you come up with all of that?" she asks.

"With what?"

"All of it." She laughs. "Your whole concept."

"I did a lot of research."

"It's kind of amazing," she says, leaning forward with her head on her hands, her elbows pressing into her thighs. "I read *Hamlet* in high school, but I would have never imagined it that way. I'd give anything to be able to create something like that. I can't imagine what it's like to be inside your head."

"Thank you," I tell her again. She looks at me like she's waiting for more, an eager interviewer, but I don't know how to react to her enthusiasm. Not only that, but how do I tell her that the last thing she could possibly want is to be inside my head? She doesn't know what she's saying. We're quiet for several moments and panic settles in my chest like oil in water. I scramble for a conversation starter, anything to end this awkward silence. I've always entered conversations dreading the moment when there's nothing left to say.

"My dad told me you never leave your house. I just thought you should know," she says, folding her hands in her lap and crossing her legs—hidden under a pair of skinny jeans.

"I bet he gets a big laugh out of this," I say. I glance around my apartment. I can imagine how it might seem like a joke from the outside.

"Not at all." She unfolds her legs and scoots to the edge of the couch. "We both think it's sad. He always talks about you being a loyal customer, but he wonders what you look like. He'll be surprised you're so young." She says this last part with a casual shrug of her shoulders and my chest tightens even more.

"So this is a field trip for you." The restlessness returns to my legs. "An afternoon at the zoo." I focus my attention on the Kandinsky, but the frantic shapes and vibrant colors do nothing for my nerves.

"Now you're just being ridiculous." She rolls her eyes, like she's reprimanding a familiar acquaintance. I don't appreciate the presumption, but the way she tosses me a relaxed grin calms me a little. I'll stay in my seat for now.

"It's difficult for people to understand." I scan the room for anything that might give away what I am—whatever that is. But the space is neat and minimal. Nothing stands out as overtly crazy.

"I can imagine. Are you allergic to the sun or something?" She's trying to figure out what keeps me here. She probably thought I was deformed, the Quasimodo of the Mile High City. People who've never met me, never witnessed this first hand, often romanticize.

"Nothing that exciting." I cross my legs, rest my arm on the edge of the table. "Sorry to disappoint."

"Have you always done this?" She pulls her legs up, folds them underneath her bottom and leans back against the couch.

"It's been five years." Why am I telling her? Maybe I enjoy

the prospect of frightening another villager. That's not really true. I'm not that kind of monster. Besides, something in her earnestness suggests she might want to understand.

"My god." She shifts as she says this. I sympathize with her discomfort. Five years is a long time. "So you just woke up one day and decided not to leave?"

"Yes and no." It'll be easier to get this right if I sit closer. I cross the room in tentative strides and take a seat on the opposite end of the couch. It takes a few moments to find a suitable position with the closed distance between us. I run my hands across the cushions, ignoring the way my entire body vibrates in close proximity to hers. I focus on the fabric and the velvety feel at my fingertips helps me breathe a little deeper. "After I graduated college and published my first book, I started spending more and more time at home. There were fewer places I could go without feeling uneasy—I don't like new people or situations. It seemed like the natural solution to avoiding those kinds of surprises."

"How'd you get to this point?" She leans in closer, bracing herself. People always want a reason. It's hard for them to understand the idea of a gradual withdrawal.

"I just did," I tell her. October 27th, 2004, only sped up an inevitable process—but I don't like to think about that part. The point is, I was always going to end up here.

"Where was the last place you went?" She leans even closer and her green eyes widen. I should have never let this conversation go on like this. It always ends here. She wants me to say I went someplace romantic, or significant, or at least out of the ordinary. She wants me to have seen something spectacular, or had some great epiphany, or even just told my family that I loved them. It was nothing like that.

I press into the softness of the couch. "To a mini-mart, for stamps."

She leans back. Her body deflates like a tire after you pull a screw from the rubber. "That's it?"

"I was out."

"No shit." She stares at the rug. "What happened at the mini-mart?"

"Nothing exciting," I say after a hard swallow. I have to ensure my voice doesn't betray me.

I will not tell her about the young man in the hooded sweatshirt, who pushed past me on his way out the door with eighty dollars of cash from the emptied register in his pocket. Or the clerk he'd shot in the chest. I won't tell her how you can't control things like that, no matter how hard you try. How after living my life in fear for years trying to avoid this exact kind of situation, all of the missed opportunities, all it took was something as stupid as running out of stamps. The only way to avoid any of it is to stay away, inside, where you have the power. You decide.

She shakes her head. "That's unbelievable."

Maybe it's the twisting panic gnarling in my chest as it always does when I'm forced to think about certain memories, but resentment bubbles somewhere deep within me. It explodes out of my mouth. "People are shit and life is easily destroyed. All this participating, interacting, whatever you want to call it, is just a way to make yourself feel better that it's all going to come to an unexpected end." The temperature in the room rises, like the atmosphere of my apartment harmonizes with this admission.

She laughs with her head thrown back. Her laughter startles me. "With an attitude like that, why don't you just kill yourself?"

To say the thought had never crossed my mind would be a lie. I've held a couple of aspirin or Advil in my hand more than once and thought about what it would be like to just take the bottle. It'd be easy enough—no one around to find me or intervene. Unfortunately, I'm scared to death of dying. That's largely why I'm in this apartment in the first place. I've never had any illusions that any of this makes a lot of sense.

I shift against the sofa. "You shouldn't give a crazy person any ideas."

She's still smiling. "Don't be such a baby."

I can see by the way she looks at me, staring so hard she could peel away the layers of my skin, that she wants to understand this. How can I help her? "As much as none of it matters, I guess I feel like I'm supposed to be here."

"Are we talking about God now?" She rolls her eyes and I'm surprised. I would have pegged her vibrancy for that of a believer. At least someone who doesn't know any better than to go on thinking the world is a beautiful place. Perhaps there's a darker shade somewhere inside her.

"Hardly." I've never been one to wrestle with the esoteric crisis. What's the point? Whether you're right or wrong about what comes after, you're still dead. I stand to check the thermostat.

70 degrees—right where it's supposed to be. Why are my cheeks so hot? "I just mean I was conceived on purpose, by parents who wanted me alive, their inherent notions of sowing the seed and perpetuating the species aside. That's reason enough, I guess." Who am I kidding? The thought of dying sometimes wakes me up at night—mid-scream—sends me into cold sweats with cramped muscles all over my body. But it's easier not to talk about that, so I sit back down and face her across the sofa.

She shakes her head again. "How do you know without being out there?"

"I was 'out there' for twenty-eight years. I'd say that's more than enough time." I'm not snapping at her on purpose. This in and of itself is unusual.

"So when I grow up and have some *real* experiences, I can be as jaded as you are." Her bitterness is more than just a reaction. Her face darkens. Maybe I've just noticed the purple under her eyes. What is she thinking about with that hardened expression?

Too much tension. I'm losing control over my space and I can't have her acting so unpredictably in my apartment. I lean against the couch and rest my head against the back, trying to look as relaxed as possible. "People do what they have to do."

"It's that simple?" Her raised eyebrows, like Romanesque arches, suggest she doesn't believe me for a second. Am I that obvious?

"It's just the way it is."

"There's nothing you miss?" She leans in closer again and her eyes narrow, as though she's studying the chinks in a piece of armor, looking for a weak spot. I didn't know we were at war.

"This may surprise you, but there's an awful lot you can do from your apartment." I wave my arm, motioning to my living space. When I say it out loud like that, I can almost believe it. Sure, I miss the experience of visiting an art gallery on a quiet afternoon or getting lost in the corners of a bookstore. I used to enjoy doing research at the CU library. But for every one thing I miss, there are innumerable other reasons to avoid the experience all together. The art galleries on Santa Fe attract a strange audience. And bookstore cashiers can be overly nosy about your reading tastes when you checkout. With so many school shootings, libraries don't feel safe anymore either. Desire has never been as strong a competitor as fear.

"What about going to a concert, or the feeling of grass against your skin, or a great slice of pizza fresh out of the oven?" She crosses the room, goes over to the window and opens the curtains. Is she showing me what I'm missing or does she just need a little natural light?

"You can get anything on DVD. Or watch it online." I come to stand beside her at the window. I don't like her changing things. I straighten the curtains but let them stay open. She won't be here forever. "Anyway, I'm allergic to grass and if I bake a pizza myself, it's fresh when I eat it."

"You're missing the point." She turns away from the window and looks at me. Our faces are close. "Those are just examples. You just miss out on the experience. Period."

"Isn't experience just another word for a mistake?" I think there's an old Oscar Wilde saying that goes something like that. We considered doing a graphic novel of *Dorian Gray,* but I was too intimidated to adapt the prose. I couldn't even begin to appreciate the decadence of that world.

She looks down at her feet, bites her lip. "You've got me there." I glimpse that brief flash of something like a shadow in her expression, as though a veil of smoke has drifted between us—a sfumato painting. "But I like to think it's all worth something."

"You're very opinionated," I say, because it's true and I don't enjoy being lectured. Who is she to tell me how I should or shouldn't live my life anyway? I get to my feet. "How old are you?"

She laughs and sits at the dining table. "I'm 25, why?"

"Just wondering what you're doing delivering groceries to the mentally ill."

"Helping my dad. I'm trying to save money—maybe start a Master's program at the University of Denver."

"What do you want to study?" I ask, in part because I'm interested, but also because I think she wants me to be.

"I did History at CU-Denver as an undergrad, but I got sidetracked." She looks over my shoulder, breaking eye contact. "I want to get my Master's in Art History, maybe do a Museum Studies emphasis."

"Are you an artist?"

"Not really," she says. "Not like you."

I focus on the rug.

She doesn't miss a beat. "But I quilt. I also embroider and knit."

Not what I expected. "What would you do with that?"

"Work in a textile arts department," she says with a jerk of her shoulder. "Or maybe run a gallery."

I try to picture her working in restoration or giving tours to groups of school kids. "I don't see it."

I shouldn't have said that. I see the hurt in her eyes. But she rallies. "At least it's something," she says.

"Fair enough." We sit for a few awkward moments, and the silence is heavy in her presence. She drums her fingernails on the table and I twitch with each sound — the ants are back, this time crawling across my thighs. Perspiration covers my palms. Light flashes in the corner of my eyes.

She takes her phone out of her pocket and checks the time. "I better go." She stands and moves for the exit.

"Just a second," I say and approach my drafting table. I pick up a large manila envelope I'd set off to the side. "This is for Angel's grandma. Could you make sure she gets it?"

There's something like surprise in the way her eyes widen, but she takes the envelope with a delicate grasp. "What is it?" She asks.

I give her a nod and watch as she pulls the drawing out as though it were centuries-old.

"Angel told me she likes horses. They remind her of where she grew up in Mexico," I say. The grayscale drawing depicts a light colored horse running through a field. The background smudges out of focus in a way that suggests the horse might gallop right off the page. It's chalk and charcoal, something I haven't worked with in a while. I crumpled several drafts and threw them away before I settled on this final piece. "I thought she might like to have it in her room."

"This is beautiful," she says. She slides the picture back into the envelope and smiles. "She'll love it." She cradles the envelope against her chest. "I'll make sure she gets it."

"Okay." I give her a quick nod. Then, I unlock the door and hold it open for her. "And thanks for the flowers, I guess." I think this is the right thing to say.

She smiles in a new way. It lights her expression a shade at a time, a sunrise instead of a light switched on. Her body swells with triumph. "Maybe they'll grow on you," she says. Then, she laughs and disappears into the hall.

Chapter 4

Monday afternoon bathes the apartment in the unmistakable gloom of something starting over again. I don't have weekends in a physical sense, because my habits are no different on a Saturday or Sunday than any other day, but Mondays still bear a particular heaviness. Perhaps it's some part of my subconscious forcing me to keep track of each new week. It's easy to lose myself in the space of my apartment, which operates on its own time, away from the ticking of the rest of the world. Maybe this feeling in my stomach, in my joints—this overall sensation of being weighted down, as though my body is full of sand—is a reminder that even here, time does go by. Or maybe it's because when I have a project with a deadline, Mondays mark the entrance of my colorist.

I'm sitting at my table, looking over my drawings. I've been working on some character sketches and I want Rick's opinion before I ink anything. I go over everything with Rick because I want to trust him to add the color the way it should be. This isn't usually a problem for us. He's colored every graphic novel I've done. He's very talented. I don't think I've ever actually told him that.

Lately, though, Rick's been getting bored. This is understandable. We've been working together for several years and not much has changed in what we do and how we do it. I'm a creature of habit, even when it comes to my work. Of course he wants to try something new. He plans to engage a watercolor filter on whatever computer program he uses. I don't pretend to understand how any of that works. Digital coloring is a reality of the industry, not an artistic decision. But this watercolor idea is an interesting concept. Not so common in our profession, as typically my detailed, hand-drawn inking takes the foreground to his large blocks of simple color. Rick wants to turn this on its head. He's changing the dynamics of our relationship. It could be great for our collaboration, but it gives me indigestion.

There's a sudden tightness in my throat, like I've swallowed something too large. I get up from the table and walk to the bathroom. The counter is empty, save for the bottle of soap by the sink and the toothbrush holder with a single blue toothbrush. I hate the idea of something meant to clean my mouth sitting in the open air, collecting dust and microscopic particles, but plastic covers are worse. They mold. I soak the bristles in mouthwash in between uses. Everything else is in the cabinet to the left of the mirror or in the drawers or cabinets underneath the sink. I grab an open bottle of antacids from the top drawer and pop three in my mouth, trying to ignore the way the chalky residue makes my tongue feel dry and polluted.

I wash the medicine down with a few gulps of tap water — acceptable for spitting out, though never for ingesting. Not without a filter. The U.S. Environmental Protection Agency has failed to adequately monitor tap water contaminants for years. No telling what I could ingest in a single swallow. I reach for the toothbrush. I used to have an electric one but I read a study that the lack of control in pressure applied to your teeth can wear away enamel and cause decay. All I need, on top of everything else, is sensitive teeth. So, I'm back with the manual.

I slather the paste onto the bristles and begin scrubbing the inside of my mouth. Brushing my teeth is like painting in oils. Everything is methodical, so the amount of toothpaste used is the exact amount needed and nothing gets wasted. It's applied to the white canvas of my teeth with precise pressure and action, with a locked wrist holding the brush at some distance from the tip. My form has always been impeccable. It's important to prevent gingivitis. It's even harder to get a dentist to make a house call—I've found one willing to come once a year for a cleaning but I can't imagine what would happen if I needed to have a cavity filled. Fortunately, my teeth have always been in pristine condition. I've inherited this from my mother. She's brushed at least three times a day for as long as I can remember. I spit the toothpaste into the sink and rinse it down. Then, I take another paper cup and rinse my mouth again. I'm in the small cabinet, reaching for the floss, when I hear a knock on the door.

I have to make sure the person standing on the other side is, in fact, Rick. Since I don't have a usable peephole, I crack the door without removing the chain.

"What's up?" He smiles from the small opening. It's definitely him. His dark hair hides under a Colorado Avalanche cap, but sticks out in haphazard tufts on either side of his head. I close the door and unlock the chain, then open it. He blazes in like a rhinoceros and I can smell the staleness of last night's alcohol oozing into the hallway around him. He could have showered. "Man, you missed one hell of a party."

I'd asked Rick to be here at ten. That way I had enough time to do my daily hour on the treadmill and take a shower before he arrived. I should've known he'd never make it out of bed before noon.

"Huh." I re-lock the door as Rick looks around. He's here often—at least once a week when we're collaborating. Not only that, but we lived together for four years when we were students at CU-Boulder. Still, every time he comes, he takes stock. Maybe he fantasizes about finding newspaper clippings from a secret life, or human heads hanging in the kitchen. I'm sure he's entertained the idea. He'd love to be acquainted with a serial killer. No one likes to tell a horror story as much as Rick. I can already tell by his excited state, the energy that grips him as he moves across the living room, he's got one for me today.

"Wish you could've been there." He lets out a burdened sigh as he drops onto the couch, legs spread. He's a less anatomically ideal, though equally licentious version of the Barberini Faun. He always wants to talk when he visits and I let him because we've known each other for a long time, and because he's tolerated a lot. He's earned it. Besides, as much as his presence annoys me, it's steady, one that doesn't cause the temperature in the apartment to rise. He's a part of all of this, even when he kicks up the rug.

"That's what you always say," I remind him. I wish I could

come up with something else. If I were to say 'me too,' I'd sound like a fake because I don't want to be at some disordered house party crowded with drunken strangers and broken glass, and because if I really wanted to be there I could be. In the end, the only thing really keeping me inside is me.

"I'm serious. It was fucking epic." He laughs and reaches up, rests his arm across the back of the sofa. His broad shoulders and wiry upper body are hidden by an oversized blue and gray striped sweater, but his khaki shorts expose his skinny legs. Men should not wear shorts. Our bodies are not aesthetically pleasing and I see no reason to broadcast this. I also wish he'd fix the corner of the rug.

"Did you take that girl?" With Rick, there's always some girl. He met this one a few weeks ago and they've slept together several times. The look on his face, his brow inclined imploringly in my direction, suggests he's blown her off and needs me to understand why. I nod along, half-interested, because talking to Rick at least provides me with validation that things could always be worse.

He shivers. "That's done, man."

I've changed my mind. Rick is really just a steady disruption. It's his calling card. He comes in with his stories and his chaos and he kicks up my rug, too swept up in Rick to even fix it. I bet he hasn't even noticed the upturned corner from his spot on my sofa.

"Really?" I sit down in a chair at the dining room table—where I've laid out the sketches he's here to review—so I'm facing him but not close enough to smell the cloud of old booze and fresh body spray. I'm trying to be courteous, even though

I don't want to hear the story, because Rick is my colorist. No, he's more than that. He's the one who takes my hand drawn art and digitizes it, cleans it up on his Wacom Intuos4. He's also my letterer. He inserts bubbles, balloons, and the scripts I create. Not many people letter by hand anymore either. Finally, he adds his distinctive brand of color both to the paper photo-copy and the electronic one. There's a whole system of color guides and computer codes, but in the end he prints the proof for my approval, and I don't ever have to worry. He knows what he's doing. Beyond all that, though, he's my friend. Has been, all this time. For that reason I can suffer the disarray a little longer. The corner of the rug is still bent over, but I don't want to move closer to fix it.

"It's too bad." He shakes his head. "She was sexy as hell. I'm talking great tits, tight ass, and hot damn was she flexible. This one time we—"

"Is that necessary?" I raise my hands to interrupt him. I don't want to hear the vulgar details. I scoot my chair closer to the table and lay a hand on one of the soft pieces of illustrating paper.

"Statement of fact." He laughs, but I can tell by the way be shrugs his shoulders, waves his large hand in front of him as though he were the Buddha making gestures of supplication, that he understands this is not something I want to hear. He's remembered who he's talking to. Sometimes Rick's showmanship must go on hiatus when the circus comes to my apartment. "Seriously though. She has problems." He lets out a loud belch, pushes back against the sofa and slips off his shoes. I cringe at the thought of his stinking carcass seeping into my cushions.

I rise and take a few steps forward to smooth out the edge of the rug. I can't let it go any longer, upturned and reminding me that others have the power to affect change, even here in my living room, that I'm not as in control of things as I pretend. I have to end this line of thinking. I won't come back. To distract myself, and because he looks at me with curious eyes, I move into the kitchen to get myself a glass of water. I reach up into the cabinet and take out the tumbler on the middle shelf, right hand side. I always use the same one. There are other glasses in the cabinet, ones that rarely serve a purpose other than to fill up space, but seeing them reminds me of Rick's presence. "Do you want something to drink?"

"I brought my own." On cue, he produces the old flask he carries around, silver and scratched, the one his father gave him as a high school graduation present. The one he duct-taped to the inside of his jeans to smuggle into the stadium the one and only time I went to a university football game, back when we were freshmen. I hated how crammed the student section was— everyone standing on the bleachers, pressed together like sardines. I thought the way everyone got their keys out and shook them above their heads to signal a key play was ridiculous. You'd never recover them if you dropped them in that crowd. I left before the fourth quarter was over, when a sloppy drunk sorority sister in a custom *Go Buffs* t-shirt so cut to shreds it was basically pieces of fabric hung over her sports bra spilled her bottle of Gatorade and vodka down my back.

I hold my water glass up to the light, looking for smudges. Then, I open my refrigerator, reaching for my water pitcher—

fresh filter replaced every Sunday—and pour myself a glass. Unusual circumstances brought me and Rick together. We were roommates, both art majors. I wanted to be a graphic artist. I'd always drawn and painted, but was new to the world of graphic novels, having been introduced by a high school teacher who took an interest in my talents and let me do an independent study on *Maus*. I knew, even then, that I'd found my calling. It might be the only thing I've ever been sure about.

Rick wanted to spend his days staring at nude models and developing a talent that would make sex more readily available. He got to do a lot of both in the art program. When he took a graphic novel class, he fell in love with the art of it. We encouraged each other's interest in the genre. We bonded over art and other similar interests, as well as a mutual respect for one another's raw talent. This respect only grew as our talents did and we began to entertain the idea of working together. It's been the two of us ever since. Sometimes I wonder if Rick ever really liked me outside of all that, in the beginning or even now, but that love of what we could create together has been enough to sustain us all these years.

"What kind of problems did she have?" I place my glass on the table, careful to keep it a safe distance from my sketches.

Rick takes another swig from his flask. From the smell of it, he's drinking whiskey. If I say anything, he'll just tell me it's an average Monday. "This chick… She had fucking issues. Like hard core shit." He leans closer so his elbows are resting on his knees; he's really worked up over this. Sometimes Rick engages in activities of a questionable moral nature. He likes to think this *joie de vivre* gives him his sensibilities as an artist. Perhaps this is why I've never had a desire to color my own work. This is also why if my colorist was arrested for drunk and disorderly conduct, it'd be a sizable inconvenience for *To Kill a Mockingbird.*

"What kind of issues?" I take a sip of my water. Then, I lean in so I'm mimicking his dramatic pose — very Rodin.

"Like drug issues. *Serious* drugs." He leans back against the couch, readjusting himself again. Happy's also always in motion. Hers is a graceful energy. He's a lumbering shadow of nerves and chaos with jet black hair. "You know I'm 4/20 friendly, and I've bucked E at the right party, but this girl has a major coke problem."

"What makes you say that?" I put my fingers on my lips, imagine myself in a shrink's office at some medical park, with a yellow pad of legal sized paper and a Mont Blanc fountain pen, talking to Rick about his sexual misadventures. I'd ask him about his parents, especially his mother, his first sexual experience — anything that might indicate why he always chooses to fornicate with such dysfunction. But I'm not in an office. I'm in my apartment, where I always am. I take another sip of water.

"Because she's fucking snorting *all* the time. She has her dealer on speed dial." He turns the cap on his flask, reaches it up to his lips and then thinks better of it. He returns it to his back pocket. "Yesterday, I came out of the shower and she's at the coffee table in my dining room doing a line and I can't figure out what the hell she's got in her hand, right?"

"Right." My water's almost gone but I'm supposed to be riveted so I don't move to refill it. Instead, I wrap my fingers around the glass in anticipation.

"Anyway, I come closer and then I see it on my couch. This white thing with a string attached. You know what it is? It's a tampon. A fucking tampon on my living room sofa." He's excited now. He lifts his butt off the cushion and resettles.

"No kidding." I cringe. Another reason why living alone has its charm.

"She's taken the pink plastic part, I guess the thing they use to push it up—you know. And she's trying to use that to snort her blow. When I ask her what she's doing, she says she spent her last dollar bill at a vending machine and had to get resourceful. Can you believe that?"

"Hardly." I shrug my shoulders—not because what he's told me doesn't have an effect on me. My skin swarms with the moist distress of considering such a discovery in my own living room. But if I acknowledge the horror, he'll want to take it further. My nonchalance might save me the agony of greater detail. But he needs to talk. He's upset and for some reason he thinks this will help. I stand with my glass in hand. Now seems like an appropriate opportunity to refill. "What did you do?"

"What do you think? I told her to get her shit together and go snort her cotton pony cocaine somewhere else."

I refill my glass. Then, because Rick's looking at me with expectancy in the upward creases of his forehead, I let out a, "Hmm."

"That's all you've got?" He sounds so disappointed.

I sit back down. Because he's chosen to talk to me about this, for whatever reason, I take a minute to think about what someone else might say to him, how someone who's better at this sort of thing might try and comfort him, or at least make him take stock. I sip my water. "That's a terrible story." I nod. "But why are you so upset?"

"What do you mean, why am I so upset? It's fucking disgusting." He takes the ball cap off and scratches his head, runs his fingers through his shaggy hair. "You can't even eat a piece of fruit without scrubbing until it bleeds. Think about it."

"But this isn't that different from some of the other times." It's not the first or the worst story I've ever heard him tell.

"I don't know." He lets out a heavy sigh and replaces his cap before settling back into the couch. "I guess I just thought she seemed normal. No spoon feeding fetishes and the sex was insane. Maybe I thought I could have it all." Rick's talking about the fact that he wants to enjoy all the steamy, sticky parts of life without the droll aspects of obligation to complicate things. He's all about the momentary pleasures.

"Maybe you aren't looking in the right places." I say this because it sounds like something Dr. Kidman would say, or a line I might hear in a movie, and I suppose it makes sense.

Rick laughs. "This coming from the guy who hasn't left his apartment in five years." He may have a point. In fact, Rick and I aren't so different. However opposite the approach, in the end we're both avoiding.

All this talk about our personal lives is wearing on my nerves. Besides, he's already dumped the woman, did it on the spot, so discussing it further is just re-experiencing. As someone who spends a large amount of time reliving past incidents, I can assure him that nothing good can come from that. But I don't want to drag that all up now. Time to refocus. "Should we go over these sketches? You may feel better."

"Don't you even care a little?" He rises to his feet and stretches, his fingers almost grazing the ceiling.

"I don't know." I immediately regret saying it.

"Ouch," he says, but he moves toward the table and is ready to get serious. For this I'm grateful. Not because I don't want to care, but sometimes I just don't know how. He begins thumbing through the drawings.

"Nice." He pauses on a full page concept sketch. "Who's this?" He lifts the piece of paper off the table and passes it to me, his eyebrows bent inward toward the bridge of his nose. I look at the sketch. It's a letter size piece of illustrating paper with a rough pencil drawing of a young woman in a Depression era house dress with a simple plaid pattern and no sleeves, just ruffles down the front of the v-neck.

"That's Mayella Ewell." I tell him like it's the most obvious thing in the world — because it should be. She's the only 19 year old woman in the novel, and the sad lines of her face, the slender contour of her body, should suggest that she's alone and longing. I drew from several Depression era photography collections for inspiration.

"What's with the hair?" He doesn't look up from the drawing. Her hair is down, and it hangs around her shoulders. Though it's a gray scale drawing, I've shaded the hair in vibrant color. I'm playing with the idea of giving her the reddest of red hair — unnatural red. Red like cherries or blood. With the dusting of gray freckles across her pale face, she looks eerie.

"Is it a problem?" I move to put the drawing face down on the table.

"You know I like me a redhead." Rick raises his eyebrows up and down a few times so he's certain I catch the implication that he's talking about sex. I roll my eyes. Rick's always talking about sex. "Just not how I pictured her. She was pretty plain in the book. Kind of heavy too." I'm always a little surprised to discover he does, in fact, read the books we adapt. I should give him more credit.

"I believe the phrase was 'thick-bodied.'" I quote the passage he's referring to. In the sketch, her head is oversized on her small frame and the lines, while life-like, are simple, almost cartoonish. In keeping with the original narrative point of view, the entire graphic novel is being rendered from the eyes of a child. It's a worldview I have only small memories of, and am either thieving or making up as I go. I've never felt so out of my element. Rick's loving it. Perhaps, I'm doing this at least a little bit for him. "And you of all people should understand artistic license." My usual sense of intricate realism is ever-challenged by Rick's desire to play with color, with the drama of our art. He adds a sense of grandiosity to our projects.

"She'll look great with the watercolor filter." He jabs at me because he knows it's killing me, this potential inking in brushstrokes, the prospect of working with different materials, a foreign sensibility to my straightforward linear style. He wants my lines to curve, to flick, to grace the page with subtle simplicity. Then, he wants the page to explode with color. He plans to, within the clickable buttons of his computer program, dab, blot, and drip color over my ink, both ignore and transcend the lines, so they are the anchor for his kaleidoscope. My eyes drift to the Kandinsky. For a depressing bildungsroman set in the Great Depression, this is asinine. I hope it works.

"I suppose she will." After all, he's good, and he's here. We're in our fourteenth year of serious collaboration. He's not family, or a friend of the family. He's stuck by me of his own accord. I should, at the very least, acknowledge that.

He sits down at the table and gets out his iPhone. He's a committed technophile. Every time he purchases some new device, I'm forced to look on in counterfeit awe as he demonstrates its awesome power. In my apartment, technologies remain basic. But photographing the sketches gives him something to take with him so he can consider how he wants to proceed when I have some finished ink. He begins laying pages out one at a time and snapping shots, holding his phone a foot in front of his face. His movements are meticulous. I stand over his shoulder and watch, in part because I'm curious to see the photos as they appear on the screen, and because I never like to be too far away when someone else is handling my work. Of course I trust him. I trust him enough to color the thing. And yet, it's as though I'm tethered to the table and every time I get too far away, the weight of the rope, the harness across my chest, pulls me back. So, I teeter in the living room, standing over Rick.

"How was Kidman last week?" Rick asks, not looking up. He's only got a few pages left.

"Fine." I cross my arms. Rick, like my parents, wants to

come over on some average day and discover that I've achieved a miraculous breakthrough.

"What did you talk about?" He always asks. Sometimes I answer. It's a delicate system we've created, in which he offers me the opportunity to give as much as I want, and sometimes I meet him in stride. Does he ever feel anger toward the skew in our relationship, the lack of balance? In all probability, he doesn't think about it. Sometimes I envy that.

"The groceries." This is more or less true. Rick shoots me a glance over his shoulder and raises an eyebrow for a moment, but I stare at him, vacant, and he realizes this is the only explanation he's going to get. He drops his shoulders, demonstrating that at least he's tried. He snaps his final photo. He must be dying to get out of here.

If I were anyone else, I would be too.

Chapter 5

The few trees I can see from my window—the ones that stand erect here and there along the river—have gone from green to shades of red and orange to nothing but branches. Mid- October. It's been a month now and she keeps bringing the groceries. Angel's grandmother has recovered. She's having the drawing I gave her framed, or so Happy tells me. Angel's returned to some of his normal routes. Not mine.

I asked Happy last week why she keeps coming back.

"I don't always know," she said. "Maybe I'm waiting for you to tell me."

I don't know what she wants me to say. Sometimes I think she's exploring my apartment, the way everything works together as part of a larger system. Here in my apartment, I make the rules. I have to. She's come to see how this all works; that it does work. I work. Or at least I maintain. Still, on the days she comes, she's always trying to implant little pieces of herself—like the vase of daisies.

Sometimes she makes slight changes in my grocery lists—a free indulgence here, an interesting kitchen gadget there. She introduced me to the short season of Honeycrisp apples. They're the best I've ever tasted. She slipped in a bottle of wildflower honey from some place in the mountains with last week's delivery — I enjoy it in my tea. When I put in a request for a new can opener, she gave me an extravagant electric one at no extra charge. I've always read these are a cesspool for germs, but this one is cordless and stainless steel and with proper care I think I can make it work. It does look rather sleek on the counter.

I notice other things too, those less intentional. I've found a few red hairs on the back of the couch when I vacuum. I pick up smells that are unfamiliar in the regulated air of my apartment. She's in a constant state of motion and her scent lingers anywhere she's been. As I touch various objects she's brought, I remember the way she's handled them, the way she curled her slender wrist in order to hold something out to me. She's always present somewhere.

Today she's here in person. She's brought my groceries and has spent the last five minutes trying to convince me not to dump a quart of 1% milk down my sink. "You can't really like the taste of that soy garbage," she said when she first placed it on my counter.

I remember drinking real milk as a child, dipping chocolate chip cookies. We always had the packaged kind because they were better than anything my mother attempted to bake. She tended to overcook everything, afraid the raw eggs would carry salmonella. I'd dunk a cookie in the milk about halfway, let it soak long enough to soften almost to the point of disintegration, and then pop it in my mouth. I loved the combination of flavors and the strange, soggy texture of the cookie against my gums.

But my mother always limited the number I was allowed to have, and I'd be left with half a glass of milk, cookie dregs floating, like debris in the Platte after a storm. My mother hated waste, so she'd force me to swallow it down, no matter my protests. I stare at the purple and white carton of milk on my island. My stomach aches at the memory and it feels like I've just scarfed half a package.

"You're being ridiculous." She breaks my thoughts. I watch her at the window.

She's looking at her nails, a gesture she manufactures not out of boredom, as I've always thought women do, but out of frustration. She's wearing short denim overalls with a white button-down shirt underneath. Her bare legs are elongated by the white heels on her feet. Her footwear for delivering groceries is always interesting. I've never seen anything like this romper and I'm tempted to ask her if she's started working for the city sanitation department, but the way the blue contrasts with her hair as she stands in silhouette reminds me of a John William Waterhouse painting—the one of Miranda from Shakespeare's *Tempest*, as she stands and watches the storm brew. Does Happy ever feel that way looking out at the frantic city? The Platte's a far cry from a powerful sea storm. Still, does she ever feel relieved to be here? Even for a second? Sometimes I wonder if that's why she comes back. Maybe she finds a small comfort in the quiet here.

"Childhood trauma can have a powerful effect on people." Back on subject: what we're really talking about is milk.

"Mommy making you finish your whole glass after a few

chocolate chip cookies doesn't exactly constitute a traumatic experience, Wes." This shortening of my name is a recent development. She takes her hand off the blind and faces me. "You want to talk childhood trauma? Try being forced to eat black pudding before you could open presents on Christmas morning because your distant relatives were visiting and Great Aunt Bedelia insisted on cooking a traditional Irish breakfast."

"What's that?" I actually enjoy pudding.

"Fried pig's blood and oatmeal, with a little mint for seasoning." She smiles at the look of disgust on my face. She knows she has me now.

"The milk can stay." I put the carton in the fridge. My story doesn't bear weight to that horrible concoction—more like the slop I've seen mushers feed sled dogs on the Discovery Channel. Besides, she won't know if I dump it after she leaves.

"Have you watched that movie yet?" She's in the living room, standing over the coffee table where a DVD in a red envelope sits in the same spot it's been for two weeks. The movie is a film version of a Frank Miller graphic novel that I made the mistake of telling her I'd read. She seemed to think I needed to see the stylized dramatization of the battle of Thermopylae on screen. I didn't really enjoy the original graphic novel to begin with.

I open a cabinet door, start to put away a box of dried spaghetti, some instant brown rice. "Haven't had time." The truth is, I've never enjoyed watching movies. Not alone. There's always something to complain about with the state of Hollywood, and it's most satisfying to discuss this with another person.

"I forget, you're *so* busy."

"I am." I point to my drafting table, covered in the usual array of illustrating materials. I've gotten enough of the visionary portions of the creative process out of the way that now I'm sketching pages for the novel itself. Rick will soon have something to do besides stink up my apartment and play his iPhone.

"Right. The big project." She crosses her arms.

I reach up and put a box of bran cereal away. When I close the cabinet, she's at the drafting table, a sketch in hand.

"What are you doing?" I rush over to her, my vision blurred. I should've put this all away before she arrived. My apartment isn't safe when she's here. I never know what she might do next.

I reach out for the paper in her hand. She pulls away and says, "I'm just curious."

"I don't—" Then, I stop. My palms are sweaty and I might smudge or rip the drawing. It's one of my Mayella sketches.

"She's pretty. Who's this?" She holds the sketch out in front of her, cocking her head and scrutinizing the drawing as though she's at a gallery opening. Something stirs at her enthusiasm, but I hate that she's seeing such an unfinished piece. A raw pencil sketch doesn't hide a lot.

"Mayella Ewell." I gulp and try to swallow back the tennis ball tickling my throat.

"Really?" She looks up at me. It's one of those books everyone reads in high school, and because she tells me she enjoys books, I'm sure she liked this one. I have another critic. "I never pictured her this way."

I look at my feet, focus on the complicated pattern of the Oriental rug, take a few deep breaths. Something about the intricacy of the floral design—the geometric figures intertwined without a flaw—soothes me. My throat begins to unclench. "I've been trying out different looks."

"Can I see?" She takes a step closer, her thin eyebrows curved upward, the sketch still in hand.

"No," I say, and her face falls. "It's silly anyway." I take a brave step forward and slide the sketch from her relaxed grip. Then, I gather the pile of Mayella drawings from the table and cradle them to my chest. "She's not even a main character. Not really."

"So why waste the energy?" She motions to the thick pile of papers in my arms.

I could tell her that Mayella's description just doesn't fit the visual aesthetic of our novel, or that the vibrant red will look better with Rick's watercolor scheme. I could tell her I felt inspired, though that would be farthest from the truth. I don't have those whimsical bouts of creativity. I just work.

I clutch the papers tighter. If I stand long enough in silence, perhaps she'll get sidetracked. She looks at me, her face ignited with interest, and I start to panic, standing here wedged between her and the table.

"I know Mayella's a liar, but she's also alone—miserable and abused." I glance down at the sketches, the intricacy of her sad expression, and it's almost as though the sorrow in the graphite might rub off on my shirt. "Maybe I just want to give her something beautiful. And not some kind of glossy magazine thing. I want her to haunt the pages." She's been haunting my drawings, my thoughts, long enough.

Happy nods. Maybe she doesn't know what to say—hadn't

expected me to get serious. "It's like you're giving her a chance to be somebody different. You're making her worth remembering." She looks away as she smiles, as though the action belongs to her and her alone. "I love how you've colored her hair. Like the red geraniums." She really has read the book.

I return the drawings to the table. They don't need my protection anymore. "Maybe this whole thing is ridiculous," I say. "If she was beautiful, she wouldn't be alone in the first place."

She laughs. "You don't really believe that."

Why does she always think she knows?

I cross my arms. "I don't?"

"Sometimes the beautiful things are the most tragic."

What can I say to that? She reaches for another drawing. This time I don't stop her.

"What's this one?" She holds up an 11 x 14 inch piece of medium surface drawing paper lined with panels.

"It's a potential scene." I've been working on this for a while. Scout, her brother Jem, and their companion, Dill, play a game where they are reenacting various pieces of neighborhood gossip about Boo Radley. Each panel shows them in a different light. Jem, who I've drawn young and athletic, hides under the steps and makes howling noises. In another panel, Jem pretends to jab scissors into the scrawny Dill's thigh—Dill who is like a duck with albino white hair. Another panel. The kids acting innocent—whistling as Atticus passes. It's meant to show the passage of time, how this game progresses over the summer. Each setting is different in slight places: the sun's position, the trees in a more advanced state of bloom. Until the last frame, where Scout stands by the Radley house — a building on the verge of Gothic, with an exaggerated frame and weeping quality, so that it breathes misery. Scout looks at the house, and the caption reads: "But, someone in the house laughed."

Happy eyes the sketch. She studies it for a few moments. "Huh."

"What?"

"It's very good. It's just—"

"Just?" This is why I never show unfinished work.

"I don't think you should say 'but, someone laughed.'"

I clear my throat. "Why not?"

"It's ominous." She bites her lip. "It shouldn't be scary that Boo's in the house watching the children play, wanting to be out there with them."

"It shouldn't?" Boo's a ghost, a specter, a child's nightmare.

"I'd say: 'And, someone laughed.' If you say 'and,' it's just sad."

"But what if he's not sad? What if he's right where he thinks he wants — needs to be?"

"I suppose you're right." She nods. "And, it's your comic. But—" She looks at me. "Do you really think that's how he feels?"

How am I to know? "I didn't write the book," I say.

She gives a solemn nod, closes her eyes for a moment. Then her lids flutter open. "It's funny, the two are kind of similar, aren't they?"

"Who?"

"Boo and Mayella." She crosses her arms over her chest, like she's hiding sketches of her own. "You know, lonely souls. Misunderstood. Carrying secrets." She blinks and for a moment

I see exhaustion in the lavender tint of the skin that puffs around her eyes. "Your story is full of ghosts."

We look at each other until the silence begins to get to us both.

She glances at her cell phone and then at me, like she's trying to decide which shortcut to take on a trail map. Time to make her exit. She heads for the door and I follow, ready to shut it behind her, but she pauses just outside, as though some invisible force holds her there. She looks at me and then over at the coffee table where the red envelope waits. "We're going to have to sit down and watch that movie sometime."

"Together?" I ask, but she's already down the hall.

Chapter 6

Dr. Kidman looks at me from over the rims of his glasses. "We're talking about the grocery girl?"

He needs a haircut. His salt and pepper fuzz sticks out just over his ears and he looks more gruff than usual. It's been a few days since Happy's last visit. I've long since dumped the milk she brought and I haven't watched her movie. Yet she continues to lurk. This is why I've brought her up.

"Who else?" These clarifying questions don't inspire much confidence in his deductive reasoning. He's no Sherlock Holmes. Maybe I'm being too critical. His commute was grueling, so he complained as he walked in the door, and the way he holds his shoulders suggests he's still jittery from the stop and go traffic. I never drove much but I hated even sitting in the passenger's seat, driving through the city. The narrow streets that run alongside the historic buildings of Larimer Square and crowded stadium walkways turn drivers into cavemen—unpredictable and aggressive. You could just as easily be shot as hit with a flying piece of fecal matter.

The Doctor wears a black sweater vest that clings to his bulk. I'm more nervous on the couch than usual because it's the spot where Happy's taken to sitting. My being here now gives her another opportunity to trespass on my thoughts. In an attempt to distract myself, I imagine how different this might feel if it were a real session in his office. The one on the University of Denver campus, where he teaches and runs his research lab. It's likely decorated in framed prints of Dali clocks or O'Keeffe flowers—something primed for psychoanalysis. Every interior accessory is some homochromous shade—nothing too startling for the depressives or too stimulating for the borderline personalities. Just interesting enough to give the students something to survey. I imagine myself in a brown leather chair, gazing up at a gigantic 36" x 54" floral depiction of female genitalia that hangs above his desk—right over his head. My stomach flip flops at the blazing imagery.

"So what's the problem?" Is he like this when he's sitting behind his fancy desk, in his ergonomic chair, discussing term papers and screening case studies? He glances down at the fancy watch on his thick wrist.

"The problem is Mayella Ewell has red hair." I draw my words out with the precision of threading a needle. I can't ignore the coincidence between the dramatic fashioning of Mayella's appearance and how Happy's hair has a Waterhouse glow in certain lighting. Why shouldn't one remind me of the other? Happy's weaseled her way into everything else.

Dr. Kidman looks at me as though I'm speaking in a foreign tongue. His idea of pleasure reading is National Geographic. I used to thumb through his collection when I was younger. I enjoyed the photographs.

"She's invaded my art." I jump up from my seat, looking down at where the rug is worn from the familiar pattern of my footsteps.

"Are you attracted to this young woman?" The doctor removes his glasses as though they're as fragile as a soap bubble. Is this to intimate the magnitude of his observation?

I stop pacing long enough to look at him. My stomach stirs against his never-ending urge to steer conversation where there's no need for it to go. "That's not what we're talking about."

"Why don't you sit down now, Wesley." He motions to the spot I've vacated on the sofa. *Her* spot. The thought sours my insides like a carton of milk left out overnight. "There's no reason to get angry."

"No reason at all," I say. I shouldn't snap, but my censure of his response gives me the mobility to make it over to the couch. I drop back onto the cushion, tap my fingers against the side of my face in an effort to refocus, wait for him to draw his official conclusion. He always pauses for just a second too long when the chance for progress looms on the horizon. He should know by now that these breakthroughs are mirages, illusions manufactured by the heat of our discussions, the controlled climate of my apartment.

"Wesley." He coos my name with a throaty sigh — like one of the pigeons that land on my narrow windowsill. I bang on my windows to shoo them away. What kind of noise would send the doctor flying? "I don't want to talk about your book right now. I'm asking you about how you're feeling."

"The only emotions I'm capable of are fear, anxiety,

depression, frustration, and the occasional onset of rage." I count them off one by one on my fingers, reminding us both we've talked about each before. "This is different." I have the proof right here at my drafting table. While Mayella is sad, there's beauty in the way I've drawn her. She's far more beautiful than she should be. I pick up a handful of the concept sketches and bring them to him. Then, I stand over him because he's not an artist and the way he rifles through the pages with his chubby fingers, he might tear one.

His forehead wrinkles as he looks at each one. "These women don't even look all that alike," he says. Why do I bother?

"Of course they don't." I wrench the papers away from him, dramatic enough to make my point but conscious of how I could bend the pages if I'm not careful. "They're preliminary sketches. I'm testing styles, trying to conceive the character. But she's there."

"How?" He places his hands together, touching his index fingers, and leans over with his elbows on his knees.

"Her wrists." I say of a close up of the girl crying with her head in her hands. Her face is obscured by the hands and the mess of hair—all penciled in color. "The line of her neck and collarbone." In this one, drawn only from the waist up, the hair is pulled back, exposing the ruffles of her house dress. "Her ankles." In this one, the figure walks in profile. I let each sketch flutter to the floor as I drop them one by one. It's a little theatrical but I want him to get the full effect.

"These details aren't so obvious." He still sounds skeptical.

"Yes, they are." He doesn't understand because he can't see her the way I do. But isn't trying to comprehend my world part of what he does? If anyone should be able to solve the mystery of my psyche, it should be Charles Kidman, PhD.

He straightens up, bristles his spine, crosses a leg. "Of all of the things we could talk about, why this?"

I know what he means. In a world saturated in overwhelming anxiety, a deep-seated fear of illness and death, panic attacks, and the occasional onset of hypochondria, the grocery girl isn't exactly DEFCON 1. Yet, somehow, she's worked her way to the top of the list.

"She's distracting." I let the remaining sketches fall to the floor. "I have deadlines— responsibilities to my work, my readers. I can't have her sidetracking me. It's unproductive." I think about her too often, even just in brief moments, little nothings as one thought leads to another and she pops into my mind for a second. It's exhausting. But it's more than that. I can't accept that my world, life here in this apartment, could ever be a part of what I'm doing there on the page. I can't let that happen. This only works because my art is not my world. It's everything my world isn't, that I'm not. It's all I have to hope for. "Maybe I should ask that she not deliver my groceries anymore," I say.

The Doctor shakes his head. "Don't do that. These drawings are wonderful. Maybe she'll continue to inspire you. Something new." When he puts it like that, I can't ignore him. He's reminded me once again that he has stuck with me because he cares. What's more, I'm supposed to want to get better, and he thinks this is a step in the right direction—wherever that is. I could tell him this is the exact opposite of what I need. That it breaks every careful boundary I've manufactured between how

I live and what I create. But the sketches are rather captivating. Maybe he's right about that at least. Besides, Happy and I have settled into a steady routine at this point. I don't need the hassle of requesting her replacement either. She'll stay. For now.

Chapter 7

It's 6:46 pm on a Monday and Rick's not due for another 14 minutes, but someone's here. I'm sitting at my dining room table, making sure the sketches for the first chapter are in order and someone is knocking on my door. According to the Federal Bureau of Investigation, a house, apartment, or condo is burglarized once every fifteen seconds. The vein in the side of my neck begins to pulse. Maybe Rick's early. But Rick's not known for promptness, and he's stopping to pick up dinner, so this is even less likely. It could be someone going door to door, though our building has a 'No Soliciting' sign posted on the front entrance. It'd have to be one of the world's most inconsiderate or oblivious solicitors. Perhaps it's a child.

Children disturb me on a number of levels. They carry about as many diseases as birds and introducing one into a controlled environment is like conducting an experiment in chaos theory. The thought that I might have one at my door, breathing a hotbed of bacteria across the threshold for God only knows what reason, makes me want to turn out all the lights and lock myself in my bedroom.

The person pounds harder—perhaps too forceful for a child.

Maybe it's one of the teenagers who covered my peephole, back with another can of spray paint. But they wouldn't introduce themselves. I cross the room. I could ignore the door but there's a determination in the knocking. Whoever it is won't be giving up. Best to just get this over with, no matter what's about to happen. Damn the superintendent for not fixing my peephole. He's going to be sorry when I call him tomorrow.

I reach out and place my hand on the first chain. A violent flash of white erupts before my eyes. I bite back the rising fear that sends shuddering ripples across my body. I need to know who it is before I even consider opening the door. This is ridiculous. If I'm about to become another crime statistic, a thirty-something shut-in robbed and murdered in his apartment, I doubt the culprit will identify himself. Then again, what if it's Rick?

"Who's there?" I shout, dropping my voice into a lower register. Perhaps this will make me sound tougher somehow.

"Open up." The voice sounds muffled through the door, but clearly female. I know that voice. I crack open the door. Happy stands in my hallway on a Monday night.

This doesn't make any sense at all.

"Hey stranger." She smiles at me as though this were one of our customary exchanges. "No way to get out of watching that movie now." She doesn't have any grocery bags with her. Her purse is hiked up on one shoulder and she has a bottle of wine tucked under the opposite arm. "Are you going to let me in?"

"Rick's coming over." He's bringing dinner and a six pack of some new beer he's discovered from a brewery down in Durango. It'll knock my socks off, he told me on the phone. If

Rick knows anything about anything, it's what constitutes a good craft beer.

She takes a step closer and puts her hand on the door. "Unlock the chain, okay?"

I follow her instructions. Then, I take a step back and she pushes her way inside. She hangs her jacket on the coat rack and places the bottle of wine alongside her purse on the island in the kitchen. She leans down and crosses her arms, resting her weight on her elbows. "I wasn't sure if you drank but this is an Australian Shiraz and I thought you'd like the label. It's a nice red." She holds the bottle out toward me.

The picture is a cartoon sketch of a Popeye-ish figure in boxing gloves. I do like the artwork but wine is best saved for formal occasions and it doesn't accompany Monday night takeout and I'm not going to drink with her. And she's put her purse on the island instead of hanging it on the coat rack where it belongs. Who knows what the purse has come into contact with outside. Women often set them on the floor without thinking. What if she's been in a bathroom stall? Now it's sitting there contaminating my food preparation space. I still don't understand why she's here. I hand the bottle back to her. "Rick's bringing beer."

She laughs. "Here I thought you'd be one of those classy wine people."

I glance at the door. "Rick will be here soon." We'd planned on going over the entire first chapter so Rick could take it and start scanning. It's no easy task. What does she think she's doing? "You should have called," I say, though even this seems unnatural. She's never had a reason to call before. Still, just because I never leave doesn't mean I don't deserve a little common courtesy.

She seems unfazed as she comes around the island and takes a seat on the couch, crossing her legs beneath her like she's an invited guest settling in for a casual evening. "Have you eaten? I was thinking we could order pizza."

Her utter lack of propriety is unbelievable. I rock back and forth on my feet. "Rick and I have work to do."

"There's this great pizza place that delivers close by. They have the best sauce—nice and sweet. You'll love it."

It's as though my lungs have been clamped in a vice and can't quite expand. The pain shoots across my ribcage. I put my hand to my chest. Rick will be here any minute and she isn't leaving. Why isn't she leaving? "Rick's got dinner," I say.

"Good. I'm starving. You think Rick will want to watch the movie too?" She thinks she's staying. She thinks we're all going to settle in together for an evening of fun. She thinks she can make decisions about what happens in my space, can just show up and I'll always be here and available because I have nothing else to do. White spots again. The pain in my chest is getting stronger and my knees might buckle. Can I make it to the table? Who the hell does she think she is? My anger gives me enough strength to remain on my feet.

I throw my arms up. "I'm not just a source of entertainment, you know?"

Her eyes widen, like she's just watched a presumed mute speak for the first time. She's quiet for a few excruciating seconds and the way she blinks repeatedly, I think she might start crying. Then, she says, "I just wanted to watch a movie."

"Why?" Surely someone could take her to a movie—buy her some popcorn and share a soda (with two straws). Isn't that what people do? On dates? I guess I wouldn't really know.

She opens her mouth to respond but there's a knock on the door. Rick's timing is impeccable. "I'll let you get that." She shrugs her shoulders like I haven't just lost my temper.

I let out an exclamation of frustration and trudge toward the door. I don't even peek before I open the chain and wave him inside, hoping that by having him here now, things will get back to the way they're supposed to be. Rick carries an over-stuffed brown bag in the crook of one arm and a six pack in the other. His purple and teal flannel hangs loose over his jeans— casual and effortless. I keep my own long sleeved shirt tucked into my slacks.

"A little help?" He bobs his head up and down, rattling the top edge of the brown sack with his chin.

I reach for the food. The tang of lamb curry tickles my nostrils. This Indian place gets great reviews. I check anytime Rick wants to add a new restaurant to our rotating take-out list. Since I can't visit myself, I have to entrust my health to the good conscience and observational skills of the online community. That's about as adventurous as I get.

Rick puts his bag down on the counter beside where I've set mine. "Man, I haven't eaten all day. Now I know what an African baby feels like."

Before I can respond, Happy inserts herself into the exchange, coming over to stand between Rick and me. "Aren't you going to introduce us?" If she were a comic book character, her speech would always have the jagged edges of an exclamatory bubble.

Rick jumps. He looks at her, and then at me, and then at her, as though he can't quite decide if he she's really there. "I didn't realize you had company."

I cross my arms. "I didn't invite her."

"I'm Happy Lafferty." She reaches out her hand. "You must be the colorist. Rick, right?"

"That's me." He nods and gives her a sloppy grin. "How do you know Wes?"

She opens her mouth to answer with something she'll think is clever, but I don't give her the chance.

"She delivers my groceries." I hate introductory small talk. I also hate how she's acting like she knows Rick. My referencing him in one or two conversations doesn't automatically put them on a first name basis. I haven't mentioned her to Rick at all.

I move to gather the utensils necessary for our dinner. I never trust the plastic stuff. Who knows who's fingered it in the basket? I make an exaggerated show of procuring *only* two sets of everything in hopes that both parties standing on the other side of the island will get the picture. They keep a close watch and I have high hopes that my intentions are understood. Rick and I have work to do and the way he watches her, she'll be a distraction to both of us.

After a moment, Happy turns her attention toward Rick. "I have this movie I've been trying to get him to watch for a couple of weeks, but he keeps telling me he's too busy. I decided I'd make him watch it with me."

Rick laughs louder than usual, throwing his head back and shaking his shoulders. He's a male peacock, ruffling his colorful feathers to attract the attention of the female. "That's very rude of you."

Happy smiles. The corners of her eyes wrinkle in agreeable creases. "I know." It's so natural, watching the two of them. Like they don't have to think about anything they say. They make it look so easy.

I've unpacked the food and set it out on the island. "Can we eat now?"

Happy faces me. "What are we having?" She bends over to take a whiff of the steam rising off the Tandoori Chicken.

Rick puffs up his chest. "The best Indian food in Denver. You're welcome to join us. There's plenty." Rick's brought Tandoori Chicken, Lamb Curry, two orders of garlic naan, basmati rice, Vegetable Masala, and Gulab Jamun for dessert—a feast. But this isn't the point. Can't they see there are only two place settings? Rick is *my* guest. He doesn't have a right to invite other guests. And Happy doesn't get to invite herself. Everything's been thrown off. My apartment's been invaded and I've lost all jurisdiction over the proceedings. And maybe I'm a little hurt that Happy didn't even consider the possibility that I could have other plans. "She can't stay. We have to work."

They look at me and then at each other as though they're defiant children trying to convince a stern parent it's the perfect night for a sleepover. Rick takes a plate and starts dishing. "Scout Finch has been around since 1960. She can wait another night." Give Rick an option not to work, and of course he's going to take it, especially when said option involves a redhead. He hands the sampling of everything to Happy and then retrieves a plate for himself. It's like I'm not even here.

I want to scream. I want to throw something at each of them. I want to kick them out. But the thought that I've lost the power over what's happening in my space makes it hard to see straight. To top it all off, I'm going to have to spend the night with Happy and Rick at the same time and watch this horrible movie. At least the beer looks promising. There's a skull on the label rolling into pins like a bowling ball—and it's a porter. While I don't drink much—never enough to lose control—it's nice to indulge every once in a while. Tonight, it seems, I'm going to need it even more. As I dish myself some curry I won't be able to enjoy, knowing there aren't going to be leftovers because we've added a third party, I have to hope a decent porter's enough to survive this.

The television sits against the far wall in a location where it can be viewed from every piece of furniture. If I appreciated television on a regular basis, it'd be the greatest triumph of my apartment's configuration. I spent a fair amount of time arranging it all, as though the creation of a normal, fully functioning living room might rub off on the owner. But I'm not normal and right now I'm barely functional. Perhaps it's less of a triumph than I thought. Our makeshift dinner party moves into the living area, ready to perch. Happy places herself in her usual spot on the couch and Rick plops down at the other end almost before she has a chance to settle. I have a decision to make.

Rick and Happy balance their plates precariously on their laps. Happy reaches over and sets her beer on the coffee table.

Rick has balanced his beer on the rug, just waiting to topple over. There's obvious utility in a table. But the kitchen chairs are also wooden, with straight backs, and for an entire movie, this might get uncomfortable. I settle for the recliner. I never sit here, but it seems like the best option. I just hope I don't spill my food. That would be embarrassing.

"Fuck it." Rick's grown frustrated with his balancing act. Holding his plate high over his head, he slides onto the floor and wedges himself in the space between the coffee table and the couch, kicking off his shoes as he goes. He takes a victorious gulp of his beer, with an exaggerated sigh to let everyone know just how refreshed he is. "Much better. God, this is good." While the floor of my apartment is more sanitary than most, I can't imagine what possesses him to sit there.

Happy nods. "It's a great beer. And you have the right idea." Now she's sliding onto the floor and setting her plate on the coffee table as well. They're both bottom feeding. She slips out of her shoes. Bare feet should not be this close to something going into someone's mouth. Now I've got heartburn—the taste of curry against the back of my throat. I haven't even taken a bite yet. "Care to join us?" She's turned her eyes on me.

"Chairs separate men from animals." I relax deeper into the cushions of the recliner. I'm staying where I am.

Happy shakes her head. "Imperceptive and culturally insensitive, but suit yourself." She takes a sip of her beer, her wrist upturning the bottle like she's sipping afternoon tea.

I'm unmoved.

Rick looks from Happy to me, before clearing his throat. Is

he uncomfortable? I'd be lying if I said this didn't please me. Serves him right for encouraging movie night. "Who's going to put the DVD in?"

For a brief flash, Happy's face ignites with an unknowable expression. My stomach lurches. "It'd be easiest for the guy in the chair, wouldn't it?"

She has me. I push in the leg rest, careful not to spill my dinner. I slide the DVD into the player and settle back into my chair. When I press play on the remote, I skip straight to the start menu. A blood stained "300" flashes amidst a stormy spectacle of lightning. This could be a long couple of hours. The other two have eyes glued to the screen as they stuff their faces. I pick at my plate. I'll admit, the beer is very good.

The movie bears a great admiration for the original graphic novel, on a shot-by-shot level, as so many of the scenes are exact replicas of the original panels. But there's something even more vulgar about seeing it in living color here on the screen. The blood, the sex, the hyper- masculinity — these things, while disturbing, are not unexpected. But the way some of the visual elements are desaturated to create the monochromatic color palettes feels alien, frightening even, in live action.

Seeing the page transferred so faithfully to the screen unsettles me. The graphic novel doesn't adapt well on film. The visual aesthetics are too different, and when one tries to mimic the other, something is lost. On the other hand, is this so different from what I do? I take pieces of great literary merit and change the game — bring them to a new audience, add my own vision. But does the significance of Sir Arthur Conan Doyle or William Shakespeare or even Harper Lee come across in my decorative pictures, my reinterpreted text bubbles? Maybe my father's always had it right—waste of talent. All I know is, I hate what I'm watching. Is that what people think when they see my books on a shelf? Maybe I need another beer.

The credits roll and King Leonidas is dead and Happy watches me uncap my second bottle. "What did you think?"

"Fine." I focus on the macabre label. Thematically, this suits the movie. It's a hearty beer, hoppy but smooth, with slight notes of coffee and even a little chocolate, and I can feel it in my whole body. I almost never drink more than one of anything, but tonight it's an odd comfort. It's time to clean up the take-out boxes. I'll ask Rick to put them in the dumpster on his way out. My neighbor takes my trash down a couple times a week. I just leave the bags outside my door. But I hate the way Indian food leaves a lingering odor when it sits.

"I thought it was great." Rick's on his feet and coming into the kitchen. "Anyone want this last beer?"

Happy gives an acquiescing flick of her wrist. "It's yours."

Rick and I have each had two. "Happy only had one," I say.

"I'm fine," she says.

This is the only reassurance Rick requires. He uncaps the bottle and takes a large gulp. "What a great adaptation. I can't believe I hadn't seen that."

Rick's a raving fan boy and I'm having a philosophical upheaval and it's all because Happy wanted me to watch this stupid movie.

I start stuffing the Styrofoam boxes back into the paper sack.

"I don't like Frank Miller."

"Too dark?" Happy's brought her plate into the kitchen and is rinsing all the dishes in the sink. "Because I've read your *Hamlet*."

"Don't do that." I reach over and turn the faucet off. As much as I hate to leave the dishes sitting dirty, I'd rather do this later when I can devote my full attention to ensuring it's done correctly.

She turns the water back on. "It's the least I can do after a nice dinner."

Rick laughs. "He's not playing host. He doesn't trust you to do a good job."

I take the plate out of Happy's hands. Her fingers are wet when our hands touch. "I just like things done a certain way."

"Guess you really didn't like the movie." She shakes her hands into the sink, sending water droplets flying. I hand her a paper towel.

"I just don't see the point in mimicking something with so little originality." I leave the kitchen, hoping to draw them both away. I want them to settle back into not touching things. "It's just a translation of media."

Rick's face lights up like a neon sign. "I get it." He laughs. "We're having an existential crisis."

"Is that true?" Happy moves into the living room and sits down in the recliner where I've spent most of the night.

Why does she do that? Change the seating? I don't want to be on the couch with Rick. I settle on a chair at the table. "Hardly," I say with a shrug of the shoulders.

Rick comes over and claps me on the back. It's a rare occasion when he has the nerve to touch me. He motions to the drafting table. "He's thinks what we do is the same thing." He's hit the nail on the head, as they say. It's good to know he understands, even if now's not the ideal time talk about it. We've both had our bouts of artistic self-doubt over the years.

I give an exaggerated yawn. I do feel exhausted by all this. Getting worked up takes a lot out of anybody. "Maybe I just want to go to bed."

Rick shakes his head. "Poor Happy just wanted to watch a movie." When I mock Rick, there's an artful subtlety. When Rick mocks me, there's never any question. He's trying to make a point, I know. "She didn't realize what she was getting herself into." He moves and plops down on the sofa. He's not planning on going anywhere just yet.

"I don't think it's the same at all." Happy gives me an encouraging smile. "Your stuff is reimagined from top to bottom. *A Letter in Scarlet* wasn't even the same point of view." I'd lent her a copy of that one after she'd returned *Hamlet* in one piece. It seems to have stuck with her. "And the *Mockingbird* sketches look totally different than how I imagined the book."

"You've seen sketches?" Rick's known me long enough to know that nobody sees the roughs. He doesn't even get a glimpse as early as he'd like.

Happy lets out a single, throaty laugh. "Not without a struggle."

"You wrestled them out of my hands."

Rick squints as though someone's just sent him a message written in Morse code and he's trying to decipher the meaning.

What mystery does he think needs unraveling? Everything with me is a struggle, and Happy always gets her way. It's not difficult to see how these two facts are oppositional by nature. But Rick's had three beers and his eyes narrow just on the outskirts of an alcoholic haze and he doesn't know Happy well enough to know any of this.

"She's very pushy." I hope this will clarify.

"I bet." He tips his bottle against his lips. It's empty but he throws his head back and proceeds to drain every drop.

We sit in silence. I guess we've run out of things to say. I look from Rick to Happy to the Kandinsky to the rug, unable to focus on any one spot for too long. This pause is not the steady, peaceful quiet of my apartment in its ordinary state of solitude or even the momentary lull that sometimes invades a conversation. Nervous energy bombards the atmosphere, makes the temperature of the room rise. It's stuffy, hard to breathe—difficult to stay still.

If I could, I might suggest we all go out for a drink or ice cream, something to get us moving—an easy distraction from our inability to converse with one another. But I'm not an ordinary host and I'm not going anywhere. I get up and move to check the thermostat. The additional presence of Happy has added an abrupt bulkiness to the air and I bump the number down to 66 degrees in an attempt to compensate. When I turn around, they're not looking at each other. They're watching me—waiting. I don't know what they want from me.

After a while, Happy looks poised to break the silence. "I think I'll call it a night." She pushes in the footrest and stands, stretching upward as she speaks. Her blouse comes out from where it's tucked in her long skirt and I catch a thin line of pale skin. "I've got to wait for deliveries in the morning. The truck comes at 6:00." She reaches up and adjusts her top.

Rick shakes his head. "That's rough." Rick hasn't been up before 10:00AM since his undergraduate years. A perk of being somewhat self-employed. He does his freelance work whenever he feels like it and only teaches digital illustrating classes in the afternoons or evenings as an adjunct. He works hard but on his own terms. Another way we're not so different.

I try not to watch her. I look at the rug instead. "Can you take that trash out when you go?" Rick gives me a look that could blister my skin. "What?" I say to him. She's leaving, isn't she?

He glances over at Happy, who's hiked her overstuffed purse up on her shoulder. "You don't have to do that. I'll get it when I head out."

"Nice meeting you, Rick." She gives him a nod. "Wes, always a pleasure." She slips into her coat at snail speed, than moves for the door. Rick's taken to glaring at me—nudging his head in her direction. He looks ridiculous. Her hand's on the knob when I think of something.

"Wait." I bolt off my seat to grab the bottle of wine from the island and meet her at the front door. "You should take this."

She puts her hand over my hand on the bottle and pushes it toward me. "Keep it."

I grip the bottle tighter as her fingers linger. "I don't—"

"For another time." She smiles. "And Wes?"

"Yes?"

"I should have called first." Then, she's out the door. I move to lock it behind her, wine under my arm.

"You've been holding out, man." Rick's gotten to his feet and watches me reattach the chain. When I turn, he has his arms crossed, a sneer playing at the corners of his wide mouth. He looks like a ventriloquist's dummy.

"What are you talking about?" I set the wine bottle back on the island. I'll have to decide on a good place to keep it. I don't have a wine rack, but it should be stored on its side. It's a screw top, but still.

He pauses. "Happy seems nice."

"Nice?" This is not the word I'd choose to describe her. Presumptuous maybe.

Rick lumbers to the middle of the living room, centered in the foreground of the Kandinsky, so that he's caught in the frenzied swirl. There's something ominous about the way the figures swarm around Rick's head. "So what's the deal there?"

"What deal?" Has he had too much to drink? Three beers isn't very many, especially for Rick, but there's no telling what he might have had before he arrived. I'm a poor judge of this sort of thing. I've been really drunk exactly three times in my whole life, all in college, and all at the encouragement of Rick. Once, my freshman year, when Rick talked me into attending my one and only frat party. It was also my one and only time doing shots of Jägermeister. I spent most of the night with my head in a toilet. I still can't think about the taste of anise without feeling queasy. The second time occurred later that year, when a pretty girl from the dorms had expressed interest in me, and

Rick thought a few rounds would help me loosen up enough to consummate the flirtation. Several shots of Jim Beam resulted in an embarrassingly poor performance for my first and last one night stand. Thank God she wasn't on our floor. The third time was our graduation. I'd be obligated to ask him to stay if he were drunk now. I'm not sure I could handle that.

He pauses. I can see in the way his face is scrunched that he's weighing some heavy thought. He takes a deep breath. "Are you two a thing?"

"Be serious," I laugh. It's a heaving sound, as nausea twists my stomach like a ball of clay. Those words have actually left Rick's mouth and he thinks they have a valid reference to a situation in my life. I haven't had a "thing" since college—a terrible mistake. Besides, when the excitement of this social experiment wears off, why would she have any reason to keep coming back? This whole interaction is nothing more than a brief detour.

He puts his hands up and blows air through his lips, like a horse. "I'm always serious."

With just Rick here, I may as well start the dishes. Perhaps that will put an end to this absurd conversation. "You're never serious," I say.

He shakes his head. "You're too serious." His voice is just above a whisper.

I don't know what to say to that. Instead, I plug the sink and begin to fill it with hot water, add the necessary dish soap. I turn the faucet to full blast, and the way the loud roar echoes off the stainless steel basin of the sink is another noise indicating the end of our conversation.

Rick stands and watches while I work. The beer's made him forget who he's talking to. For a minute, he's imagined he's with another friend. A real friend. A normal one. He can see now that he's not going to get anywhere with whatever point he's trying to make tonight. He clears his throat, let's out a phony cough to signal we are changing subjects. "Did you want me to start coloring this damn novel or not?"

He could've brought that up before I added dish soap.

Chapter 8

Happy's in my apartment again, this time on a Saturday morning, a day before she's supposed to deliver my groceries, and seven days after Halloween. I don't participate in trick-or-treating, not that anyone would come to my door anyway, but I always order a couple of bags of candy just in case. It would save me the awkwardness of having to turn away a child. I don't eat processed candy — too many unhealthy ingredients. I usually send it home with the Doctor or throw it away but I was going to offer the bag to Happy. It hasn't snowed yet, not so much as a solid frost. This is unusual — even for Colorado. The strangeness of the weather, so unseasonably warm, has me on edge.

"It's too early for wine," I say, as I finish locking the door. She called first this time, asked if she could stop by. My stomach squirms thinking about why.

"What?" She sounds dazed as she sits on my couch, playing with her necklace. The pendant is a sterling silver tree she slides back and forth, willing it to fly off the thin chain and plant itself here in my living room. What a silly idea. A living thing would never be at home in here.

I sit on the edge of the couch, unable to settle into the cushions, because her unease is making it difficult to relax. My palms itch with a film of nervous condensation. I ball them into fists and rest them on my thighs. "You didn't come for your wine?"

She told me she was leaving it for another time. It's been resting on its side, wedged between the microwave and the bread box, waiting.

"Oh that." She laughs, but the sound is unfocused, like the noise is just a habit. "Not today."

"I see." The air in my living room gets stuffier by the second. Damn this Indian summer.

I get up and check the thermostat. Still at 70 degrees. Like always. At this time of year, it's impossible to regulate the indoor temperature—what's happening outside is just too difficult to predict. Even with windows, walls, and doors, the weather seeps inside. I'll leave the thermostat alone for now.

I return to the couch. "So what're you doing here?"

She's still playing with the necklace. "I have something I need to talk to you about."

My stomach lurches forward like someone's just slammed on the brakes of a careening vehicle. The way she yanks her pendant back and forth along the silver chain suggests she's about to drop something in my lap I don't want to hear. What could she have to tell me? Is she sick? Moving? If I keep losing all my delivery people, I may have to start looking for a new store.

She isn't saying anything. She's staring at the carpet— preoccupied.

"So…" I wish I knew the right question to ask. I lean down with my elbows on my knees and wait for her to speak. I can almost hear the grating sound of the pendant scratching against the chain each time she slides it. Her fingers, the thumb and pointer, grasp it with an admirable delicacy, like she's in the process of folding tiny slips of paper, an origami crane against her chest.

"So…" She sounds as mystified as I am.

She hasn't moved, save for the back and forth as she tugs on the necklace. It's as if the ebb and flow of her hand guides her like a piece of seaweed caught in the waves, moving her toward a decision.

The silence eats away from the inside, like a rotting tree. I'm not equipped to handle this. "I'm not sure what I'm supposed to do here."

She nods her head. "I know." Of course she does. She takes a heavy breath. She's poised, shoulders slumped and head down, like the self-conscious angel who mourns in Victorian cemeteries—so unlike the woman who's been imposing herself on my apartment for the past month. "There are a lot of things you don't know about me, Wes."

"There are a lot of things you don't know about me," I say. Why should this matter? An extensive background check isn't technically a requisite for our weekly transaction. Besides, I'm not the most willing candidate for proffering information. When I think about it, Happy doesn't blossom with personal narratives either.

"I'm sure." She drops the necklace and folds her hands in her lap.

I've been so focused on her damn necklace, I haven't noticed the darkened spot on the side of her face. It's a faded shade of purple and yellow, muted with a thick layer of cover-up, but not hidden.

"What's wrong with your face?" I trace the outline of the spot on my own skin to make sure she knows what I'm talking about. Perhaps an ambitious stock boy overshot his target and struck Happy with a piece of flying produce.

She cups her cheek and her whole body tenses. "I'll tell you everything, if you let me."

This openness startles me. "Okay."

She clears her throat. "You know I really want to go back to school."

I nod. We've discussed this before.

"Money's always been tight, even with the store, and I came back from Europe with absolutely nothing." She looks past me, somewhere distant, and that familiar shadow clouds her expression. "I was completely broke when I finished school and I couldn't find a decent second job that let me keep hours at Dad's store. But I had to stay. Dad needed me." She draws her words out like they burn. "I'd already started having to pay off loans—25 years old and still living at home. I was drowning."

Rick went through a similar struggle when we were in school over a decade ago. It's almost unfair that my father paid for my education in full. Look how far it's gotten me.

"Anyway, I met this guy. Lee." She flinches just a little when she says his name. "He seemed decent, kind of charming—he liked me a lot. We saw each other for two months before I moved in. It was so fast." She shakes her head. I never knew Happy lived with someone — a man. I shouldn't be surprised. Of course she has a boyfriend. "He worked at this place, The Dollhouse." She stares at the rug like she's afraid to look up. "He thought I could get a gig there if I was willing to audition. His boss, Ray, gave me a job and I've been working there ever since."

My forehead creases. "Someone let you be a stripper?"

I think this is what we're talking about. I've never been inside one of those places. My nostrils sting just thinking about the mixture of sweat, aftershave, and alcohol that must saturate the stale air. The sight of the one off Evans, with its tasteless, two-tone stucco and broken down awning, used to make me nauseous. But from what I've witnessed on television, unless you're Demi Moore, most strippers are either very blonde or very alternative looking. Happy doesn't fit.

The stripper in question looks at me with an expression that reminds me of the time I told Dr. Kidman his daughter was a little chubby for ballet. "If you actually thought about the words that came out of your mouth, you might not sound like such an asshole."

Offending her wasn't my intention. I search for the most reassuring words. "I'm sure you make a fine stripper."

"Ugh." She reaches up and knots her hair in her fist. "That's not really what I do, you know?"

"It's not?" I guess I'm confused.

"No." She releases her hair and takes a deep breath. "It's a fantasy fulfillment club. They offer a number of… services. Private striptease, role playing, fetish play, tease and denial…."

I hold up my hand. "What do you do?"

She bites her lip. "It's sort of like voyeurism?"

"*Like?*" A peep show is a peep show, right?

"What I do is a little different." She crosses her legs. She's put thought into this explanation. "I'm alone."

"And someone watches you through a hole in the wall," I say. Everything about this makes me sick. But I bite back the sudden urge to use the restroom, to relieve myself of this information, because for some inexplicable reason, Happy thinks I need to hear it, and that seems important.

She rolls her eyes. "Two-way mirrors."

I take a hard swallow. "What do you do while they watch?" This is the million dollar question. Do I want to know the answer?

"Wear lingerie and read aloud from erotic fiction."

She can't be serious. But I look at her, the way her eyes have a watery glaze, and I know she is. "People pay for that?"

"Absolutely." She nods. "Sometimes they even request a type. Corsets and Marquis De Sade or chaps and western romance novels."

I let out a sigh. "That's not so bad." I'll give her that much.

Relief brightens her expression. "I never take my clothes off and I can't see or hear them. They pay to sit and watch and listen in the privacy of their own room with a plush sofa and the freedom to do whatever it is they do."

"Gross." I don't want to think about that. I have a feeling there's a little more to it, how she reads, but I guess it could be worse and I don't care for the details.

Her shoulders fall and she closes her eyes. "What am I doing here?"

"What *are* you doing here?"

She shoots off the couch like a bottle rocket and begins to pace. "It's complicated, but basically, Lee's a fucking psycho. He has some drug problems, you know? I guess I thought maybe I could help him or at least I could overlook it, but he was jacked up the other night and asked me if I'd ever considered taking my job to the next level—whatever that means. I told him he was freaking me out and he went ballistic. Said I never support him. That I think I'm too good for what I'm doing even though I made the choice." She's talking fast. "He said a lot of things. I had to end it. I called Ray and quit. Now I don't have a job or a place to live and since my dad thinks I'm working as a nanny, I can't go home." She stops pacing, stands in the middle of the room, facing me, her back to the Kandinsky—and looks at me with huge, expectant eyes.

"I'm sorry," I say. I am. I'm sorry to hear that Happy's gotten herself into such a situation. It sounds terrible. Though it sounds like it's over now. There's still one question that needs answered. "What about the bruise?"

She touches her face. "Lee wasn't very happy when I left."

This new revelation stirs a different kind of tightening in my chest. "What does your father think happened?" I don't know why I say this and I regret it when I see the way she closes her eyes tight, like she's just been slugged again.

She reaches up and touches the spot. "I was playing baseball with the kids I nanny."

I think about the panel I've drawn—where Tate remembers the bruises on Mayella. I considered drawing a flashback to show her mangled body but I didn't want to exploit that violence. Besides, the worst damage is always done behind closed doors by the people we're meant to trust. Happy seems so composed, like this is just another day. What would she consider out of the ordinary?

I decide to return to my original question instead. "But what're you doing here *now*?"

She laughs like she's laughing to keep from screaming. "Because, stupid, I need a place to stay."

I'm on my feet. "You're kidding."

She can't think our burgeoning association, let alone my living situation, makes her request even slightly possible. I can't believe she has the nerve to ask. I need some water. The flashes of light tease their way into my vision and my throat cracks when I swallow.

She jerks her shoulders upward. "I'm kind of desperate."

"I'll say." I slam the cabinet door.

"It'd be temporary." She comes into the kitchen. "Maybe just a couple of days."

"Don't you have any friends?" I try to focus on inspecting the tumbler for spots, but I can see her face through the distorted view of the glass — her expression is broken.

I've been harsh. She's scared and I've over-reacted. Of course she isn't staying, but I could say it in a nicer way. It's not you — it's me. Cliché but so true. I open my mouth to apologize but she straightens up, cuts me off.

"I do have friends. But nobody knows about this. I'm only telling you because you're not a friend. You're not anything."

So she hasn't been seeing all this as the start of a lifelong camaraderie. Though, if she didn't like me just a little, why'd she make me watch that ridiculous movie? Regret stirs in the way she leans her head to the left, bites her lower lip.

She starts to say something but I cut her off. "Rick's not your friend. Stay with him."

"I'm not going to stay with Rick. I don't even know Rick."

"You don't even know me."

She crosses her arms. "I know enough. You're different."

What's that supposed to mean? I take a gulp of my water. My throat stings. "Why here?"

"It's safe. No one will find out. No one would think to look."

I know what she means. From the outside, this apartment may as well not exist at all. Nothing occurs to remind the world it's here.

She catches my gaze and holds it. "Just until I can figure something else out?"

"Absolutely not." I slam my glass down, a little harder than I intended. "This is so inappropriate. I should call your father."

"Jesus Christ, Wes. How old are you?" She's leaning against the island, her weight on her hands. The curve of her body relaxes but her voice is strained. The way she looks at me, the way she talks to me now, makes me feel ridiculous. "I'm asking to sleep on your couch for a couple nights. I'm not messy. I'm a good cook. I won't even be here during the day because I'll be searching for a job and a place to live. I'll pay rent. Whatever."

"What about my groceries?"

"The *groceries*, Wes?" She crosses her arms. "We can figure something out."

We both know she's right. I should've led with something else. "I just can't." I start pacing in my kitchen. "You don't understand."

I feel like a lion stalking the perimeter of its cage. A familiar pain creeps along my ribs and takes hold of my chest, like my body's being held in an iron embrace. My heart races—it could rupture at any second. I brace myself against the counter, put my hand to my chest. I try to take a few deep breaths but the pain is too much, the muscles too unyielding. The light flashes white hot.

She sees what she's doing to me, takes a few adventurous steps, reaches out a hand. I want to recoil, but she squeezes my shoulder and her touch eases the pressure just a little. She's going to tell me she realizes her mistake. She's going to tell me how foolish she's been and that she's sorry and we can go back to sharing conversation over delivered groceries and maybe another movie, but that is enough.

"Please, Wes?" She leans over, looks me in the eye, and the rounded lines of her forehead are pleading. "I know it's a lot to ask, believe me. If I had another choice, I'd never have even gone here. But you're sort of my best option."

I manage to let out a constricted laugh. "That's pretty sad."

She gives me another one of those halfhearted grins, like she doesn't have the energy to curl her lips all the way. "Yeah." She bites the bottom one again. "It is."

She moves her hand to my back and rubs it in a circular motion. My mother used to do this when something frightened me as a child. I always found it calming. When Happy does it now, it makes my muscles tense. "You don't know how embarrassing this is for me."

I can only imagine. I'm mortified.

I straighten up. Never in a million years would I have considered this. I wouldn't have even thought about it. I wouldn't have taken time to weigh the pros and cons, as I am now, leaning against the counter in my kitchen. Happy claims to be clean, and she's definitely well put together, so this could be true. And, she's grown up in a grocery store, so maybe she can cook. She'd be sleeping on the couch, which wouldn't be a total interruption to my evening routine. It could be an inconvenience if she sleeps late in the mornings, but as she said herself, she's going to be trying to find a job and a place to live. She may be getting up earlier than I do. For a few days, I could make this work.

What am I thinking? She'll have to share things. She'll be in my bathroom — my shower. She'll fill my free space with her belongings, no matter how temporary. Who knows what she might try and bring into the apartment? There's no way of predicting what conflicts may arise, what disagreements we may have. It's a disaster waiting to happen. No one's ever stayed here. Not even Rick. Granted, if he was just too plastered to make it home and his killing another person driving under the influence weighed on my conscience, I'd let him stay. But Rick would never allow himself to be in such a state in my apartment. No one would allow themselves to have to rely on me. No one asks me for anything. Why would they? Yet here she is, asking me for something now. She's asking me to be the kind of person she can rely on, the kind of person who has the power to help. Maybe that's the reason I'm going to agree.

Chapter 9

It's 5:00 pm and I've called Rick to tell him he better not come over tonight.

"Is she there now?" I can hear the concern in his voice, but I wonder who he's really worried about.

"No. She left. Said she had some business." I'm standing in the kitchen. A large suitcase, hot pink with geometric shapes of white and purple, rests against the couch. It looks like the luggage of a twelve year old girl. The way one of the wheels has broken on the bottom and drags along the floor, it could be that old. There are others too. A matching set. She told me she left them all waiting in the car on the off chance I'd agree. This irks me, that she even thought I might. The tote sits on the counter in the bathroom. This large one sits by the sofa, staking claim to what will become Happy's bed. I don't like it. It's an eyesore.

"What kind of business?" He sounds conspiratorial.

"I don't know."

"You didn't ask?"

"No." The suitcase is the most hideous piece of luggage I've ever seen. Even worse than the black duffel Rick ripped on a trip home to Oregon during college and had to duct tape back together to make it through the airport. "None of my business."

"Hey, man. When a doll moves in, everything's your business."

A doll? Rick must've been watching old movies again. Or is he poking fun at Happy's previous profession? Maybe I shouldn't have told him. "I'll keep that in mind."

I hear a heaving breath on the other end of the line. Rick's preparing himself, going to give me one of his "friend" lectures. I definitely shouldn't have told him.

"I just—"

I hear a knock on the door.

"I have to go. We'll reschedule for later in the week."

Then, before he has a chance to say anything, I press "end" and slide my phone back into my pocket.

I move around the island and stand at the door. This is it. Once I let her in tonight, she's here to stay. Just for a few days, but that's enough. I reach up and unhook the chain without asking who's waiting. I'm slipping.

"Why does it take you so long to answer?" She has a brown cardboard box in her arms.

"What do you mean?"

"I can always sort of feel you on the other side of the door." Then, because I look at her like she's been talking to the voices, "Not in a creepy way, just how you can sense people are in proximity sometimes. You never answer right away."

I reach out to take the box. "I was trying to decide if I should let you in."

She lets go. "Well, thanks."

The box is heavy. I slump with the weight of it. Happy moves to throw her purse on the island. Then, she hangs her coat on the rack. I set it down so I can hang her bag. She never learns.

"What is that?" I motion toward the box.

She nods her head. "Come here, I'll show you."

I take a few steps to where she stands at the kitchen table, rummaging through the contents of the container.

"I had to go by The Dollhouse today." She looks up at me, her hands still in the box. "Pick up some things."

I should have asked before I touched the box. My hands feel dirty. I thrust them into my pockets. "How did it go?

"I just picked up my stuff and got the hell out of there." She reaches up and touches her face. The bruise on her cheek has faded to a faint yellowish brown. It'll be gone in a day or two. "I made sure to go when I knew I wouldn't run into anybody I didn't want to see."

"What did you take?"

"Mostly books." She laughs. "I used to pick them up at garage sales or thrift stores."

That explains why that box was so heavy. She holds up a couple volumes. One has a plain white cover with golden letters and a white horse—how elegant. Then, there's a Harlequin cover featuring a half-naked couple on a pirate ship. The man has long, blonde hair and black leather pants, not to mention washboard abs to rival a Wolverine comic. The woman has fiery red hair and a pink dress, corset bursting.

I cross my arms. "Classy."

"Pirate romances are intense." She laughs. "The pirate king

kidnaps the governor's daughter and seduces her aboard his ship, where, after she's given the greatest pleasure of her life, she teaches him how to be a gentleman. Or something like that."

I flip through the pages, try to imagine paring this prose down into some kind of manageable, graphic form. So many adverbs. "They call this fiction?"

She raises her hands. "I don't write the stuff."

"No, but you read it." Out loud. To men behind a two-way mirror.

"It's not like I read the whole thing." She starts flipping through the pirate book as if this proves something. "I just skim for the relevant passages and dog ear the pages."

"Those are a lot of bent pages."

"Some books are better than others."

There's something I'm curious about. "Do you have any favorites?"

She shakes her head. "No."

"Yes, you do."

She bites her lip. "I don't."

I pull out a chair and sit down. "You're telling me you don't have a single text you enjoy reading more than the rest?"

She gives a close-lipped smile. "I guess if I had to pick one, it would be this. It was never very popular with the customers."

She hands me a book. I recognize it as a title of Anais Nin erotica. The cover is a photograph of a 1940's woman pulling up her dress to reveal her thigh. I flip it over, look at the back cover. It's an older edition, could even be a first edition paperback. I flip open the cover to look at the copyright. 1978. It has that musty smell of an older book. It's distinct, something to be remembered, but it also lingers in my nostrils, makes my eyes water. It's a smell I can never decide if I like.

"Why this one?" I ask her.

"I don't know," she says. "I like her style, I guess. I wish I could desire something even a little like she does."

"I haven't read it." I don't want her thinking I know what she means by that. I flip through the pages—quite a few are bent. I should have known this is how she treated her novels. I can't believe both of mine made it back in one piece.

"You shouldn't do that to the pages." I hand it back to her. "This is an early edition. It could be worth something."

"Thanks." She puts it back in the box. Then, she looks at me with an eyebrow raised. "You're not going to ask me to read you something? Show you what I do—or used to do?"

"Of course not." I take a step backward. "Why would you ask that?"

Her eyes spring wide in uncertainty, but she looks down at the floor. "I don't know, I just—"

"'You just' what?" Does she think I'm the type of person who could enjoy that? What does that say about me?

"Nothing." She laughs to herself, shakes her head, closing her eyes for a brief second. I can't imagine what's funny. "Have you eaten?"

"What?"

"Dinner." She points to the kitchen as if I didn't know that this is where the food comes from. "Do you want some?"

"I guess." She did claim to be a good cook and it's been a

long day. I'm too tired to fight her. I can supervise.

"Okay." She moves into the kitchen and takes inventory, removing food from the pantry and fridge. She pulls out a box of rice, starts boiling water. She works with the confidence of someone who thinks she belongs there, at least for the time being. She believes she knows what she's doing. It's likely I won't die from anything she fixes.

"I'm going to scour some of those online job boards tonight after dinner. I'll try to do some applying in person tomorrow. Face-to-face is always better, don't you think?" She looks at me, then turns to the stove, where she proceeds to pour vegetable oil into the wok. "I guess you don't have to worry about that." She's begun to chop a red pepper, which she mixes with broccoli and spinach from the fridge, then she sets the vegetables aside and pulls out the flank steak I'd been planning on eating tomorrow. She cuts the meat into thin slices.

"You need sheets."

She stops cutting and looks at me. "What?"

"For the couch," I say. "I'll find you some. And a blanket."

"Thanks." She adds the meat to the wok and the oil crackles. I think she's making stir fry. "I want you to know that I'll be out of your hair as soon as possible." As the meat sizzles, she mixes a small bowl of soy sauce, garlic powder, dried ginger, a little sugar, and some crushed red pepper flakes from somewhere in the back of my pantry. Between adding each ingredient, she lifts the wok from the heat and gives it a ferocious shake. She throws the vegetables into the wok and the ripeness of the peppers mixed with the meat makes my nose itch.

My stomach objects to watching someone else prepare my food and I taste acid in the back of my throat. I try and focus on something else. "What time do you think you'll be home tomorrow?"

"Why?" She pours the marinade into the wok. It crackles as she coats the vegetables and meat by tipping the pan in a circular motion.

I can't watch. I move down the hall and into my bedroom. I go to my dresser and open the top drawer. In the back, there's a small metal box with a combination lock. I turn the dial, and slide the lid open. When I return, Happy stands with her hands on her hips, having just removed the wok from the heat.

"If you think you'll be home before six, you can have this." I put it down beside the stove.

She looks at it and then at me. "A key?"

"It's a spare."

She bites her lip. "I don't think—"

"That way you won't have to bother me to let you in. Just make sure you're not out too late. I can't leave the chain unlocked for very long after it gets dark. It's not safe." I collect plates for the both of us.

Happy checks the rice, which has been boiling for a while now. Then, she takes the key and slides it into her pocket. "Thank you, Wesley."

I move for the kitchen table with two sets of silverware. "Make sure the beef is cooked all the way through."

After dinner, Happy asks if she can take a shower. I get her a clean set of towels and clear a space under the cabinet for her to keep a few toiletries. I leave when she turns on the water and sit down at my drafting table. She takes a long shower, over twenty minutes. I try to ignore the sound of the running water, but I can't. When she appears a while later, she's wearing gray sweatpants and a blue t-shirt made to look like the Colorado state flag. She's wrapped her hair up in a towel. She comes and sits on the couch.

"That felt good," she says. Then, she pulls the towel off her hair. It falls limp and wet across her shoulders and droplets of water dampen patches of her t-shirt a shade darker. She combs her fingers through the tangles. "Nothing like a hot shower to help clear your head."

"I'm glad," I say with a nod. This talk is painfully small. It seems neither one of us is sure what to say now that we've settled. The conversation at dinner was just as awkward. I took to lecturing her on the importance of low sodium soy sauce. I'm about to tell her she should be careful sleeping with wet hair because it causes the pillow to mold, but she speaks first.

"I almost forgot." She gets to her feet. "I brought you something." She goes to her suitcase, which is still sitting at the end of the couch. I will have to find a place for her to unpack in the morning. Maybe I'll clear a shelf in the hallway closet. She stands up and presents me with a folded quilt. "I thought it might look nice on the back of the couch."

I take the quilt and unfold it, lay it out so I can see the whole thing. It's what's called a crazy quilt—an intense and vibrant pattern of colors and textures, with random fabrics sewn to create individual blocks which are pieced together with over-exaggerated cross-stitching in thick red embroidery thread. I like the way the oddly shaped pieces of fabric are laid together to form something completely new. The color combination, the energy, makes me think of the Kandinsky.

"Did you make this?" When she told me about her love of textiles, I'd imagined simple block patterns quickly sewn together by a machine. Not this.

She stands at the other end and smiles. "Do you like it?"

"Yes." I pick up two corners and prepare to fold it. Happy picks up the other end and we bring each of our corners together, folding the quilt in half. Then, we walk toward each other and meet in the middle, folding it once more. I take the quilt from Happy and lay it over the back of my couch, just as she suggested. I think I could get used to having it here, even after she goes. "You're right," I tell her. "It really brings out the colors of the painting."

"I think so," she says. Then, she sits down at one end of the couch. She leans over and pulls her laptop onto her crossed legs. "It's one of my best."

"Thank you," I say, because I do like it and nobody has ever given me a homemade present before and even if she didn't make it for me she gave it to me and something about that makes my face flush, like the pleasant heat just before a sunburn.

"Thank *you*," she says, and then her head disappears behind the glare of her computer screen. I take one more look at the quilt before I return to my drafting table.

Chapter 10

I wake up because I'm dying. My heart races so fast it might tear out of my chest. The sheer weight of it presses against my lungs. I gasp, thrash my arms and legs, manage to throw the sheets from my body. It's unbearable to swallow, as though my throat's a section of PVC pipe. I try to scream but the noise is the faint echo of a voice through a tin can phone. It's freezing but I'm drenched. What's happening to me? Heart attack? Stroke? All I know is, this is the end. I'll die alone in my bed. At least Happy will find me in the morning. If she wasn't asleep on my couch, it might be weeks—the stench of my decomposing body seeping into the apartment below me, the neighbor's complaint to the super. The pain in my chest is like the impact from a wrecking ball. The room slants. Do I have regrets? Soon my vision will darken, and that will be it. Could I have done more? In some ways, I've always known this is how it would end. Even when the desire to leave has torn at every part of me, dropped me to my knees at my own front door, in the end I'm the one who can't, who doesn't just take the steps. I'm the one who's made it this way. I can't be better, so here I am. I'll die alone in my bed.

The light flips on. Happy stands in the doorway. "Jesus.

Why are you screaming?"

I screamed? Out loud? "Can't breathe. Heart attack." I sputter, grabbing at my chest.

She comes to the bed and crosses her arms. "Are you sure?"

Am I sure? "I'm dying."

"Try and take a deep breath."

Call 9-1-1! Her questions waste precious seconds. The average response time to a 9-1-1 call is over four minutes and I could go into cardiac arrest any second. 23% of heart attack victims die before reaching the hospital. But I manage to draw in a mouthful of air, swallow it down. I do it again, in sync with Happy. She's making dramatized motions of inhaling and exhaling in her oversized t-shirt and yoga pants. Something shifts in my chest, loosens just a little. I sit up. And think, not again.

"Better?" She asks after we've done a few more cycles of breaths together.

"I'm okay." Just another panic attack.

The gentle arch of her eyebrows, soft lines at the corner of each eye, pity me. That makes me ache a little more. "Can I get you anything?" She says it like she's talking to an old man with emphysema who's just undergone a coughing fit.

"No." She doesn't have the lease on my dignity.

She shrugs. "Some tea?"

My impulse is to get her out of here so I can pull the covers up over my head and never come out again. Still, tea does sound soothing. The hot liquid might loosen the mass in my chest. I nod and straighten the sheet around my legs. "With some of that honey you gave me."

She moves for the door.

"Hey, Happy?" I reach out my hand, just as hers touches the wooden frame.

"Yeah?"

I push myself up a little higher against the backboard. "I really thought I was dying."

"I know." She pads down the hall.

I started having night terrors when I was five. I'd jerk awake, wide eyed and screaming, in the middle of the night. My mother said it was a macabre sound, not quite right for a little boy — a noise my body shouldn't have been able to produce. I'd spend several minutes gasping for air, moaning, sobbing. I was inconsolable, though never even fully awake. After some point, I'd lay my head down for the rest of the night. In the morning, my father would interrogate me but I could never remember. It terrified my mother — the helplessness of not being able to control my outbursts. My father never came to my bedside. He said it was a normal part of growing up. Maybe he just didn't want to feed my mother's worry — a conflict of parenting. It went away after a year or so and that was the end of it. Now it's panic attacks. I started having them in high school, every few months, brought on by particularly stressful situations like finals or my driving test. The frequency only increased through college and then after. Now they're a part of the regular routine. I'm most afraid of dying when I'm alone at night. Imagine that.

Happy's back in no time. She must've found the electric kettle. "Here you go." She sets the mug on the nightstand. "It's the lemon one you had in the pantry. Hope that's okay."

I wouldn't have gone with a citrus flavor this late at night—always risky for heartburn, but I wasn't specific. "That's fine."

She teeters above me for a moment and I can see the indecisiveness in the way her shoulders stiffen. Stay or leave? She sits at the foot of the bed, her body in slow motion, like the mattress were a piece of inflatable furniture. She's in for the long haul. I pull the sheets up further, tuck them just below my arms. After I'm comfortable, I reach for the tea. The mug is especially hot between my damp fingertips.

She folds her hands in her lap. "What was that all about?"

I shrug. "I have panic attacks." I blow on my tea. "They're worse at night." It's important for her to think this is nothing. I don't want her to worry that she's spending the night with Woody Allen. No reason two of us shouldn't be able to sleep.

She flicks her nails so they make a *click click*, bites her lip. "And the dying thing?"

"That's what triggers them." I take a sip of my tea. "I have a fear of dying."

She smiles. "Don't we all?"

I put the mug on my nightstand. Too much honey. "I guess mine's a little more intense."

"This happens a lot when you're here alone?"

"Yes." Obviously. I'm always here and I'm always alone.

She adjusts. "How often?" Her hand is too close to my foot, which is hidden under the covers.

I cross my legs. "It's hard to say." At least once a week.

She wants to tell me how sorry she is, I can see it in the glossy finish of her eyes. She resists. "So, you just lay in bed, thinking you're dying until it goes away?"

She makes it sound so dramatic.

"Sometimes it's not this bad." I cross my arms, look her straight in the eye. I need her to believe this next part. I don't want her to be scared, not because of me. "I get up and walk around, calm myself down. Or I get a glass of water, go back to bed. Tonight was rough." Though not the worst. It's been a few years since I've called 911. "It's the one negative aspect of my living situation."

"The *only* one?" She laughs.

"Yes."

"Oh." She's thinking now. I can see it in the way her forehead creases, like she's trying to remember the answer to a particularly difficult question. "Does it have to do with what happened at that mini-mart?"

"What?" I ask. I was careful not to tell her anything about that.

She gives me a sheepish look. "Something happened, right? I could see it in your eyes." She's suspected all this time and hasn't pressed. Now, she wants to understand. Maybe she thinks this is the key to understanding all of it, to understanding me. If only it were that simple.

"I've had issues a lot longer than *that*." I look at her. We're very serious now. "That was just the icing on the cake."

"Will you tell me?" she asks.

When she says it like that, what choice do I have? I close my eyes, take a centering breath. I have to find the right words to explain the situation without recalling too much. "I came in as the shoplifter left. He'd shot the clerk. The man didn't make it."

I'll spare her the details, how I found the clerk shot and bleeding behind the counter. I hopped over, whipped out my phone and dialed 9-1-1. The man's head rested in my lap as the red blood spread out across his white dress shirt. I tried to tell him it would be okay. He opened his mouth to speak and the blood gurgled from his lips. Tears teased the corners of his squinting eyes. I cried too. I wished, prayed, that someone would come. Then, he sighed heavy—a deep, burbling breath, and his lungs filled with blood. He died. I closed his eyes with my trembling fingers as sirens blazed into earshot. There's no sense, no justice, in something like that. It could have just as easily been me.

Happy is quiet for a long time before she says, "You talk about it like it's no big deal."

"It is what it is." Nothing and everything—whatever.

"It must have been the scariest moment of your life." She swings her legs onto the bed and faces me, pulling her knees to her chest and wrapping her arms around them. "It would've been for me. I'd have spent a lot of time going through all the hypotheticals." She runs her hand along my gray, micro-plush blanket. "What if I had bought stamps another day? Gone to another store? What if I had come in just a few minutes before?"

Three rather distressing questions. I can't talk about this. The thought of it, the memories, all those feelings of anger and dread that always simmer just under the surface, now threaten to break through the thin layer of my skin. I feel them burning. If I let the panic take hold again, I won't have the energy to fight back. All this pillow talk belongs in someone else's bedroom. "It's getting late," I say.

She sighs. "So it is." She stands and moves for the door. Then, she turns and faces me again. "Thanks for telling me," she says. "I'm really sorry you went through that."

"Thanks again for the tea." A redirect. I can't talk about that anymore. I lie down and pull the covers up just to make sure we're clear that I'm done talking. "Good night."

She gives me a tentative smile before flips off the light. "Sleep tight."

Chapter 11

Happy sits on the couch, eating a bowl of my vanilla Rice Dream. She's wearing her gray sweatpants and Colorado t-shirt again and is watching Thursday night television. She's been engrossed in a prime time drama—something medical. She's knitting something while she watches—a shawl, I think—and I'm amazed at how fast she works. She never seems to look down. Her hands move with a mechanical sense of purpose. I'm at the kitchen table, inking a scene where Atticus shoots a dog on his neighbor's behalf. It's a chance for Scout to ruminate on her father's age, all the things she doesn't know about him, and it's an opportunity for me to get a little dark in the surreal child's view I've been drawing. I've been avoiding this scene. This change of pace would be welcome under different circumstances, but to really capture the violence of it, to do it justice, I have to call on experiences I've already been spending too much time thinking about lately. I can't create these frames without those memories finding their way onto the page. This scares me more than anything.

Over the last few days, Happy and I have stayed out of each other's way. She's gone before I get up, working early mornings

125

at her father's store. She's been going around to various businesses, handing out resumes and collecting applications. She's hoping she can piece together an income between her hours at the grocery store and another part-time job. Yesterday, she came home around lunch and I made her a sandwich. We've exchanged phone numbers and sometimes she texts me, lets me know what her plans are. We've been making dinner together, because I don't enjoy feeling useless in my own kitchen and it's good to keep an eye on what she's doing. She's proven herself more than adept, but you can never be too careful when it comes to raw meat. We haven't spoken much since dinner tonight— chicken and grilled vegetable fajitas— since she's relaxing and I'm trying to work. Every now and then something on the television makes Happy laugh. The sound forces my eyes up from my illustrating paper.

"Sorry," she says, a residual giggle escaping as she speaks. I shrug my shoulders or roll my eyes. Sometimes I'll let out a "humph," if her laugh is too loud or distracting. Then, it's back to depression era Alabama for me, and sex-crazed doctors for her.

We stay like this, in a tenuous balance, until there's a knock on my door. Not a knock, a pounding—an angry pounding— like someone expects confrontation. This is strange. Maybe the superintendent has finally troubled himself to replace my peephole. It's only taken weeks of aggressive messages. But it's almost 9:00 pm—not an appropriate time for maintenance. Besides, he'd call first.

"Are you expecting someone?" I glance over to where Happy sits cross-legged on the couch.

She stares back at me with an unspoken apprehension, her eyes wide like a police officer's shining a flashlight in her face. She shakes her head but gets to her feet and moves to place her bowl in the sink.

She looks at me. "Well?"

She's right. No use wasting time. The person on the other side of the door is impatient. Looking through the peephole is like looking through a camera when the lens cap is still on, but I do it anyway. The pounding intensifies.

"I know you're in there." A male voice hollers from the other side of the door.

This isn't happening. I run my hand along the chain to make sure everything is locked and put my back to the door like my thin frame could barricade a person trying to enter. "We shouldn't answer," I say. We should call the police. We should imagine nobody is out there. I glance in Happy's direction but she isn't looking at me. She's looking past me at the door.

"Lee?" she calls, and strides to where I'm standing. The look on her face, it may as well be Frank Castle on the other side.

"C'mon, baby, let me in." So this is the ex.

"No fucking way," she says, waving her arms in front of her as though he could see her through the door. She took the words right out of my mouth.

"We shouldn't wake the neighbors." He talks fast, like a cartoon character who's had too much coffee.

"Shit." Happy's voice cracks. She clears her throat. "How the hell did you find me?"

"Followed you back from the store."

Perfect. She's brought him right to my doorstep. I run my palms against the grain of the wood, remind myself how thick it is, how sturdy. I'm safe on this side. "Can we make him leave?" What I mean is can she? It's her fault he's here.

She looks at me. "What do you think?"

"We should call the police." I pull my phone out of my pocket.

Happy shakes her head. "And tell them what?"

"We should do something." My intestines are on fire. I could keel over from the pain.

She sighs, bites her lip. Then, she reaches out and touches my arm. "I think we have to open the door."

"Are you insane?" My voice is half-way between a whisper and a shout. I push myself away. "Maybe you should go out there and talk and talk to him."

"You can let me in now or I'll come back. It's up to you. I know where you are now, Happy."

Happy's cheeks have a pastel glow. "Let's just get this over with."

I take a step back. I'm saying neither yes or no, washing my hands of where this will go. I don't want him here in my apartment. I also don't want him lingering in the hallway. He might decide to break in or something. From the way she's described him, he seems to do whatever he wants without a second thought. What's to stop him? I could call the cops, but he'd just leave and come back later. I need this to be over now. Happy reaches up and unlocks my door.

"What the hell are you doing here?" she says, taking a step back as he crosses the threshold.

The ex-boyfriend is tall, well over six feet, with light brown hair gelled to have a look of purposeful disorder. His face, unshaven, is half hidden behind a pair of Ray Bans — laughable at 9:00 at night. He wears a sky blue sweater vest over a striped button down shirt with dark jeans and startlingly white sneakers. Something about this getup makes me like him even less. He fidgets, crossing his hands in front of his body. Sweat beads along his hairline.

"Who the fuck is this?" He jerks his arm toward me.

"Wesley." It takes all the breath I have to spit my name out. My voice sounds like a deflating balloon.

Lee cocks his head and narrows his eyes in my direction, like he's trying to read some kind of tiny message on my forehead.

Happy comes to stand next to me, arms crossed. Her face has ignited in a deep flush. I can't make out her faint freckles underneath the red. "That's none of your business, Lee."

He lets out a staccato laugh. "Nice to see you too, hot legs."

That's interesting. I've always found Happy's legs a little disproportionate to her body.

"What do you want?" Happy asks.

"I've missed you." Lee lets out another strained laugh, like someone's just slapped him too hard on the back. He reaches for her.

She takes a step back. "Just stop."

I'm lost in my own apartment, a stranger to the events transpiring here. My head starts to spin as I watch the two of them standing and staring at one another. His hand jerks up with unnecessary aggression to wipe his nose and I remember what Happy said about the drugs. How did Happy end up with someone like this? She spent over a year of her life in his apartment, in his bed. And here he is now, uninvited. I have to regain control of my space.

"What's going on?" I'm surprised by the boldness in my voice.

So are they. Two heads snap in my direction. Now they remember where they are.

"Should we sit down or something?" Lee says and drops down on the edge of the couch without waiting for an answer. Happy looks at me. She's waiting to see what I'll do. I want to ignore his suggestion, tell him he has some nerve dictating what we should do, but my legs tremble like I spent an extra hour on the treadmill and I need to sit. I give her a small nod and sit down at the kitchen table. She pulls out the chair at the other end. Lee produces a crumpled envelope from his back pocket. He sets it on the couch beside him. "I swiped your last paycheck off Ray's desk. He was going to mail it to the grocery store but I thought you might need it."

Happy looks away from him. "I'm surprised you didn't try to cash it," she says.

Lee twitches his legs back and forth, unable to sit still. He leans forward and looks at her. "C'mon, babe, cut the bullshit. You know why I'm here."

She holds out her hands, palms out. "I have no idea what you're talking about."

"I miss you." Lee shifts against the couch, as though the cushion's leather that's been sitting under the sun. "I don't want to get into this in front of this guy."

"I told you it's over." Happy's voice rises in pitch.

"Just like that, huh?" Lee's shoulders tighten and he jerks upright. He looks from Happy to me, his eyes settle on my face. "Please tell me you're not fucking this guy." He looks at me as he says this. He doesn't look away when I think he should. I glance down at the rug, focus on a series of shapes along the edge.

"Fuck you," she says. Her anger startles me. "What are you on right now?"

Lee jumps out of his seat like something's bitten him. He towers in front of Happy. "Just come talk to me." He grabs her arm and tries to wrench her out of her seat. "I just need you to talk to me."

"Don't touch me." She kicks him in the shin. His arm snaps backward. Is he going to hit her?

I'm on my feet. "Stop." My voice cracks but I say it loud enough to get their attention.

Lee gives me a threatening glare. "You don't want to get involved here."

Happy flashes me a look, her uncertain eyes twisted in the deep lines of her face. For a second, I think she might actually go with him, she's considering the option. Maybe she thinks this is easier for me, for everyone. I could let her out the door and lock it behind her. But she might not come back. Her eyes are pleading. She doesn't want to go. I muster up enough courage to bite back at the snarled thorns of my abdomen, giving myself a quick slap in the jaw, refocusing the discomfort. Lee looks at me like I'm crazy. Maybe this gives me an edge.

"She doesn't need to go anywhere if she doesn't want to."

I cross my arms, stand tall, try to make myself look bigger, like they tell you to do with black bears or mountain lions, other predatory animals. My stomach knots itself tighter and I don't know how long I'll be able to stand up straight. "You should go now."

His expression shifts. It's hard to tell from under the sunglasses but the hard crease of his forehead suggests rage. "What did you say?"

I'm almost doubled over. "Leave now or I'll call the police." I motion toward the front door.

"Wouldn't that be stupid," Lee says. Then, he looks at Happy. Some of the color has returned to her face. She crosses her arms and nods.

He puts his hands up in some kind of gesture of defeat. "Okay. I get it."

I follow him so I can lock the door as soon as he's gone and barricade it with a chair. Happy's right behind me. He has his hand on the doorframe when he turns around. "Come on, Happy. We can figure this out." He reaches out and grabs her arm again, tries to tug her along with him.

"Let go," she says, swatting at him with her free arm.

"Enough." I reach out and slam my hand down on Lee's arm, like a karate chop in a Bruce Lee film. I'm not sure why I choose to strike him this way, it just happens, like my arm does it without consulting me.

Lee releases Happy and stares at me for a second. Before I realize what's happening, he winds up and my left eye explodes in a spasm of pain. I rock back several steps, grasping at my eye.

Tears fill the one I can still open.

Happy rushes to where I kneel in the doorway. "Jesus Christ, Lee!"

"Be seeing you," he says to one or both of us, and he's out the door.

I'm seeing white spots, different from the ones I've seen so many times before. They spin, frenzied, like I'm on the verge of losing vision altogether, or maybe blacking out. I have to sit down. But the door is unlocked.

"Go." I point toward it until Happy gets the message. She hurries to lock it. While her back's turned, I tumble to the bedroom and lock myself inside. It's a smaller space, with another lock, and being on this side of the door loosens the lumps in my stomach. I fall on my bed and face the ceiling. It's plain and off-white, a flat surface, with a thin crack in the paint that runs along the middle, right above where I sleep. I've stared at this exact spot many times before. Nothing's changed here in my bedroom.

Happy's rooting around in the kitchen, opening drawers with a loud clang. Then, she gets into the freezer. I catch the sound of clinking ice. Is she fixing herself a drink? Perhaps she found the Johnnie Walker my parents gave me for my birthday last year. "It might loosen you up a little," my father had laughed. He knows I never drink hard alcohol.

Happy tries the lock. It almost turns, but it holds. "Come on, Wes, open up."

"No thank you." I close my eyes. This seems to dull the pain in my face—not enough, but it's an improvement.

"I've got some ice."

Ice. I hadn't thought of that. I've also never been punched in the face before. I imagine the cold against my skin. It would be good for the swelling. But I don't want to see her right now. She introduced that animal to my apartment. She brought the world to my door. "Go away," I tell her.

She knocks again. "Dammit, Wes. Open the door."

"I don't want to."

"Will you please just let me in?" She starts knocking. At first, I think she's kidding. Not kidding, but not serious. She begins with a one handed rapping at a repeated interval—slow and simple. If I stare at the crack in the ceiling, I can ignore it. As the second hand crawls around the face of my wall clock a few times, she gets frustrated. The pounding intensifies, becomes more rhythmic. She begins a two-handed beat, steady, as though she's playing a djembe against my bedroom door. I watch the crack in my ceiling, that soothing image, but it blares out of focus. She pounds and pounds and my head throbs and my face aches and her frustration only makes me feel worse.

"Fine." I'm on my feet and at the door. I unlock the knob and return to my spot on the mattress.

She has a bag of ice cubes in her hand. She comes across the floor with her head down, like she's marching to a funeral dirge. She sits down at the foot of the bed and hands me the Ziploc. "Here."

The ice has begun to melt. Tiny droplets of water condense along the outside—cold against my fingertips. "It's wet."

"Really?" She scoots closer and rips the bag away. "Let me

see." Bending over, she takes my hand, peels it away from my eye. She stares for a minute before she says anything. "Oh God."

It must look promising.

She presses the ice to my face, so gentle she might be reaching out to touch a stray dog. Neither of us speak. Neither one of us knows what to say. Her fingers graze my forehead. The sensation of her fingertips on my skin draws the feeling away from my eye, refocuses it. I let my head press deeper into the pillow. I close my eyes. The ice numbs the throbbing to a dull ache and after several minutes I'm feeling good enough to sit up.

"Well, that was fun." I right myself and take the ice from her.

She sighs next to me. "I'm so sorry."

"You should be." My face is killing me.

She looks down at the floor.

So much for my apartment being the last place on the face of the planet anyone would look for her. I shift the ice against my face and it sends a stinging sensation across the bridge of my nose. "What did he even want?" She shakes her head. "I really don't know."

This next question is of great personal interest to me. "Do you think he'll be back?" The thought makes me shiver — maybe it's the ice.

"I think he made his point." The corners of her eyes droop in an apologetic frown.

I'm sorry to have snapped at her. She had as little control over what just happened as I did. I should lighten the mood, for both our sakes. "Your ex-boyfriend has a solid right hook."

She attempts a smile. "Was that a joke?"

"I guess."

"Maybe I should get you some Advil." That might be the best thing she's said all night.

She hops to her feet and disappears into the hall. I'm not sure she knows where to find my supply, but I'm too tired to show her. I lay my head back and close my eyes. She reappears moments later with a glass of water and a couple of pills in her small hand. I take the pills and swallow them down. This should help. Now, if only I had something to make the panic go away. This hooligan knows where I live and could come back at any time to finish what he started. What was started tonight? Right now, I don't want to think about it. I want to curl up in my bed and hope that sleep finds me in spite of all of this, but I look at the circles under Happy's tired eyes and I remember this all happened to her as well. On a level I can't begin to understand.

"Are you okay?" I ask her.

"I'm fine." I hear the conflict in her voice. She's upset, scared. But, she's said she's fine, and I want to respect her answer.

I give her a nod. "Okay."

"I just can't believe he came here." So she does want to talk. She lifts her legs onto the bed and pulls them up against her chest, so that her head rests on her knees. The last night she sat on my bed like this, she comforted me. "He had no right to show up here. I thought I was done with all this shit."

"Can I ask you something?" I press the ice harder against my face.

"Sure."

"Why did you date him?"

"I don't know." She shakes her head. "It's a problem I have."

I take the ice away from my eye. "What kind of problem?"

Now she laughs, but it's restrained, sad even. I worry I've stopped respecting some secret boundary between us, but she answers. "It seems I'm only attracted to a certain type of man."

"Why?" She's so bright, I don't understand this shade of her.

"It's exciting, I guess." She shifts against the mattress. "Or it's always about the sex. Or because my mom died when I was young. Lots of excuses. I guess I'm damaged goods."

"Does this happen often?"

She shrugs. "It's happened enough. Though Lee takes the cake."

"I'm sorry," I say. I'm sorry people have hurt her and that she seems to think she deserves it. The way she looks, so raw and vulnerable, like unfired clay, makes me reach out and rest my hand on her shoulder.

She's surprised at first. She glances in my direction, eyebrows raised. But she relaxes, rests her head so her cheek is against my hand. Both of us are shaken by tonight, and while neither of us want to say it out loud, we can sense it in one another. So we sit, only just touching, only just comforting, but together. It's a strange connection. An unfamiliar one. We stay like this for a long time. Then, she straightens.

She's looking at me now. "Hey, Wesley?"

With these two words, the entire atmosphere of the room shifts. The fear's still present, but it's bombarded with other feelings, pushed and pulled out of focus. The air tenses with another mood. I try to ground the fear, to fight the atmosphere, because my face still hurts, and I'm going to have a black eye to remind me of how very real this anxiety should be, but I'm being pushed and pulled as well.

"Hmm?"

"Thanks for sticking up for me tonight."

How do I respond? If I say, "no problem," this isn't true, because it is a problem. I got punched in the face. If I say, "it was the right thing to do," I sound like an asshole. If I say "anytime," the situation might arise again. None of these things are quite right. I shrug my shoulders.

"No, I mean it." She reaches out and puts a hand on my arm. "That was big of you. I want you to know how much I appreciate it." A part of me wants to throw something at all this sentimentality, but I won't. I shouldn't. My stomach swarms like a can of worms.

"Okay," I nod. It's an acknowledgment. The best I can do.

"Okay." She smiles, brushes a piece of hair out of her face with a wide stroke of her wrist.

I watch her for a minute, try to understand what she's thinking. But she eludes me. She starts to squirm, bites her bottom lip. Then, she stands. Before she has a chance to go anywhere, I say, "Don't take this the wrong way, but you're better than all of that." I'm surprised to hear the words slide off the tip of my tongue. I am not this kind of person—so bold. This admission is uncharted territory.

She looks at me and lets out a close-mouthed laugh, shifting her feet and crossing her arms against her chest. "Why would I take that the wrong way?" She takes a step toward me. "That's sweet of you to say."

If invisible boundaries did exist between us, I'm not sure what they are anymore. I need to get control of this situation, of myself. "Look, I don't want you getting the wrong idea and—"

"The wrong idea about what?"

I'm weary of the glint in her eyes. My skin itches like I've just put my face in one of those old push pin art toys to leave an impression.

"About all of this. You staying here, us talking like this—"

"Do you think you might ever kiss me?"

My jaw drops—a daft expression—the kind you expect from Archie or Jughead. This is exactly the kind of entanglement I've been trying to avoid, the kind of complication I fear more than a lot of others, and now I'm forced to do the only thing I can. I lean over and press my lips to hers. It's brief and tepid, and I'm too uneasy to pay attention to whether or not I enjoy it. I pull away and look at her.

She shrugs her shoulders. "I thought you'd try harder than that." She's underwhelmed. Of course she is.

I want to tell her I'm sorry, that I haven't done anything like this in a very long time. I want to tell her that it's not that I don't want to kiss her. I do. That I know. I want to reach out and cup her face in my hand, to feel her warm cheek against my palm. But I don't. "I'm sorry," I say. "I take it back."

Bitterness replaces her playful tone. "You can't."

"Why not?" This seems like a reasonable question. Though I think I already know the answer.

"Because I like you, you neurotic fuck." She reaches up and

twists a large strand of hair in her fingers, gives it a tug. "And now I know you like me too." She lets go of her hair, crosses her arms. "A second ago, I was considering how much I'd like to…" She lets out an exasperated sigh. "But you're just so God damned difficult."

Well, there you have it. She's laid this out across the small amount of space between our bodies. I'd have put the information out with caution, like antique lace. Happy throws it down like a plastic tarp and there's no going back.

"I'm willing to give it a try." I can let go of the fear, give into this, to her. I lift my hand and brush a piece of hair behind her ear.

It's a small gesture, but it's enough. She reaches out and takes hold of my shirt, pulling me toward her, kissing me with an open mouth. I meet her in stride. I taste her bottom lip with my tongue. I raise my arms and find my way to her back, running my hands across the contours of her shoulders, down her spine to her waist. My body trembles, reacts to her soft curves as she presses against me. I want to touch her, trace the figure I've been watching for weeks. I want to be out of my head completely.

She breaks away and smiles. The slight indentations on either side of the corners of her mouth are a little more pronounced against the rosy flush of her cheeks. I lean in to kiss each one, unsure what will happen when my dry lips touch her soft skin. When she takes my hand, I follow without question, without hesitation, and without entertaining the many ways in which this situation could end in disaster. For the first time in a long time, I don't think at all. What a strange and wonderful sensation.

Chapter 12

"You aren't the only guy this has ever happened to." Happy has the sheet pulled up just over her breasts. Her blue bra straps stand out against the pale gray of the knit sheets. We've been laying here beside each other, both on our backs, staring up at the crack in the ceiling for what feels like forever but has actually only been a maximum of five minutes. Ten minutes ago, I was lying on my back in nothing but my boxers with Happy pressing against me so that her hip bone dug into my side. I felt an eager resolve as I kissed her, let my hands explore her body, grasped at the bare skin of her back.

I pulled away long enough to ask: "Are you on birth control?" I already knew that she was because I'd seen the pack of pills in the drawer in my bathroom but I needed to ask her anyway.

"Yes." She sighed and shifted against me and I knew how much I wanted her and I thought that we were going to do this. I was going to do this. Happy rocked her body against mine, our damp skin sticking like plastic melted together under extreme heat.

I groaned and said, "We should use a condom." The pill is only 99% effective and that's only if the woman takes it at the same time every day and doesn't take anything that might make it work less. Plus, the pill does nothing to protect against diseases.

"I don't have one," she said and went back to kissing.

That's when several thoughts came into my head in no particular order or perhaps all at the same time:

What if she has an STD?

When was the last time she was tested for an STD?

Has she ever been tested for an STD?

Did she brush her teeth after dinner?

What if she's repulsed (both from the standpoint of aesthetic standards and personal taste) by my naked body?

What if I'm repulsed (albeit unlikely) by hers?

What if I can't perform adequately?

What if I can *only* perform adequately?

Should I have showered first?

Should I have asked her to shower first? (She hasn't showered since last night)

What if she wants me to do something I don't know how to do?

What if she wants me to do something I don't want to do?

What if she wants to do something I don't want to let her do?

What if I shouldn't do this?

What if I can't?

What if all I am is a disappointment?

All of these thoughts built up and solidified into a heavy weight in my chest and I began to sweat and the white spots appeared and didn't go away even after I closed my eyes. Five minutes ago, I took three distinct actions. One, I stopped kissing

Happy. Two, I twisted out from under her body. And three, I said "I can't do this." Now the silent staring.

Finally, she rolls over on her side. She reaches out a hand and tries to rest it on my leg, as though I've just failed an exam or gotten a bad report of some kind. This is too much.

I lift the sheet and roll over so I'm facing away from her. I've been intimate with two women in my entire life: my embarrassingly brief one night stand during a wild night in the dorms and a nine month period in which I dated a girl named Sophie from one of our art classes and let her down a number of times before she moved on and started dating someone else. The third time, it seems, is not the charm in regards to this particular issue.

"Come on, Wes. You were nervous. It's okay." Now, her hand's on my shoulder. "We can try again."

Now she's just being cruel.

"No thank you."

She takes her hand off my shoulder, slams her arms against the bed. The mattress bounces. "That's it? One false start and you're over it?" She throws the sheet off her body. "I thought there was more to this."

She has her feet off the side of the bed. I can tell by the way the mattress creaks and the weight shifts that she's going to leave. She'll return to her couch, or worse, and this brief interlude, an inexplicable change in the dynamic of our already complicated situation, will take a step backward, reset just a little. That would be best. I'm sure of it. I should let her go.

"Wait." I roll over and reach out for her arm. "Stay."

She looks at me but her eyes are vacant. "Why?"

She's going to make me say it.

"I'm sorry. It's been a long time and I don't think… Can we just lay here?"

Her expression wrinkles in confusion, like she can't quite understand what I'm asking her to do. But her body relaxes and she reaches out her hand. She pulls the sheet back up and climbs beneath it again, rests her head on the pillow so that we're facing one another. She reaches out a hand and touches my cheek. "Okay."

Later, I watch her sleep. It's dark but the full moon blankets the bedroom in silver light and the thin skin of her eyelids are like opals. Deep creases between her eyebrows suggest a restless sleep. A nightmare? Maybe she's dreaming about me. Her bra straps stand out against her bony shoulders. Even in the dark, with strands of red falling across her forehead, the contrast resonates with a peaceful kind of beauty, like she might not wake up. She might stay like this forever. Maybe it would be better if she did. What happens in the morning? What will I say? What will she do? I don't know what any of this means, or if it means anything at all. In fact, there are so many reasons why this can't ever mean anything because I'm not capable of letting it. Maybe she's not either. Maybe it doesn't matter. I look at the clock on my nightstand, 2:00 am. Maybe it's too late to worry. It's already tomorrow.

Chapter 13

I don't care for comic strips. They're sometimes amusing and I can appreciate the talents of the Bill Wattersons of the world, but overall they're not my style. Rick, on the other hand, loves them. While he enjoys several, he finds few as inventive as Dilbert. I suppose there's an element of truth to Dilbert that speaks to the reality of a white-collar engineering office micromanaged by a moron. Others take solace in the comic strip because they know Scott Adams understands them. Rick loves it because it's a world he'll never have to know. I remember something Adams said once, about how creative people make mistakes, but artists know which mistakes to keep. Relationships aren't so different.

It's about making the biggest mistake of your life, the relationship itself, and then spending the rest of your time trying to manage it. I have been attempting to keep this mistake under control for the past week. This mistake sleeps in my bed, and makes dinner in my kitchen, watches television on my couch, and does laundry in my apartment basement—my pick-up service is too expensive.

She's staying. We talk and we kiss. We argue and we agree. We sit and we sleep. I ask her about her family. She tells me about her childhood and I'm curious to know how it compared to my own. We talk about how her mother died in a car accident when she was only a few years old, how it's been just her and her dad for so many years. How she grew up in the grocery store, surrounded by people, always spending time with teens and adults who worked there. Her companions have always been older. We talk about growing up an only child, of missing someone you can't even remember, and I see that she knows what it is to be alone.

Every day is different. Just as new patterns begin to emerge, she changes the game. And as much as this upsets me, as sick as I feel every time she turns the key in the lock, I persevere. And I think she does too. She's enjoying the newness, not just of this relationship, but of this kind of relationship. She's enjoying "taking it slow." At least she says she does when we're in bed together and I have to tell her again that I just can't—that I want to, but not yet.

It's the middle of the afternoon, and she hasn't come home yet. She's alternating days between her usual hours at the store, and a brand new position at an independent hobby store. She doesn't always enjoy it, but it's legitimate, and she gets a discount on supplies. It's as close to curating a textile department or running her own gallery as she's going to get. At least for a while. Her first paycheck should help her disposition.

She's at work now, but I'm not alone. Dr. Kidman's here. This is his first visit since she began her stay. I asked him not to come last week. I wasn't ready. Besides, I didn't want him to see my eye. It's still a faded bruise, somewhere between yellow and brown. Thank goodness Happy's is already gone or we'd look like twins. Still, it's faint enough he might not notice. Anyway, he's preoccupied. He looks around like he's hoping to catch sight of some small proof of her presence. An article of clothing left carelessly in the hallway, a pair of shoes by the door. I don't blame him. I've had a hard time believing it myself.

He sits in the recliner, one gray pant leg crossed over the other. His dark sweater covers a white dress shirt and a navy blue tie. He's come straight from the university, as usual. "Where's your guest?"

I smile. "At work. She'll be home soon."

"I'd like to meet her." He crosses his arms as he speaks. Maybe he thinks I've made her up. He should look in my bathroom. She keeps leaving her hair curling iron out on my counter.

I shrug my shoulders.

He leans forward and puts his hands together. "How *are* things, Wesley?"

More direct than usual, but what does he expect me to say?

"Fine," I tell him. Anything more isn't his business.

"No, really." He peers at me over the rim of his glasses. "How is this going?" He motions around the room, as if to indicate that 'this' isn't natural. He wants me to know that he's concerned. He wants me to tell him my secret fears and resignations, to bare my soul. He wants me to tell him that I don't know how this is going, not really, that I try as hard as I can not to think about it, just to enjoy it while I can. That when I do start to consider where this all might end up, I'm seized with the crushing weight of the idea that, at some point, she's going to leave. He wants me to say that I wish I could get up and go with her, take her on a proper date, buy her a coffee or a nice steak, but I can't. So I don't say anything for a while.

"Well?" he asks, raising his eyebrows. You can take the doctor out of the practice but you can't take the practice out of the doctor.

I cross my arms. "It's fine." This answer worked so well the first time.

He sits back, relaxes into the recliner. He can see I'm not going to admit anything. "I'm glad." He shakes his head. "How long is she staying with you?"

"We haven't really discussed it." It's an interesting question. Exactly the kind of thing I don't want to think about. He's implying that she's taking advantage of the lonely shut-in—free room and board. She hasn't mentioned her apartment search in a while. Maybe this is why I'm afraid to bring it up myself.

He takes his glasses off and looks at me. There's a gravity in the way he moves, his stare. "Is this a good idea, Wesley?"

He talks to me like a child—maybe one of his. "Is what a good idea?"

"Letting this woman stay here?" He looks around and leans in closer, as though she might have bugged my living room. "I know I encouraged you to keep interacting with her, but you don't really know her."

"I know enough." I know a whole hell of a lot more than he does. Since we're not sleeping together, we talk. A lot. I know all about her high school and college years. The alcohol and drugs. I know about why her past relationships haven't worked.

I know that despite this she continues to put herself out there in the world only to be crushed over and over again. I know that she's the first person in a long time I've really cared about disappointing. Still, I shouldn't mention anything about Lee. Or the police.

I waited until Happy left the house the morning after Lee came to the apartment. I knew she wanted to move past the night's events but I couldn't. I wasn't sure how to go about it. I'd called 9-1-1 from the apartment a few times before. Once, about two years ago, I thought I was having a heart attack. The paramedics tried to insist that I go to the hospital. I had to sign a waiver releasing them of any liability if I didn't go and then turned around and died. My father had to come and look over the document. Trying to avoid a similar situation, I got on the Denver Police Department website and read through the list of possible crimes to report online. Vandalism, identity theft, lost property, theft/larceny, theft/larceny from a vehicle, or vandalism to a vehicle—all terrifying to think about, but not exactly applicable to my situation. Then, I saw the number to call in anonymous tips.

A fast-talking woman answered the phone. "DPD anonymous tip line."

"I need to report a violent crime."

"What's the nature of this crime, sir?" I could hear the sound of her typing in the background.

I reached up and touched my swollen eye. "I was punched in the face."

She stopped typing. "Sir, you need to call the non-emergency line and file a police report. I can give you the number."

"But I'm already talking to you. I was punched in the face in my own apartment."

She let out a long, ragged sigh. "Can you identify the suspect?"

"Of course I can. He's—" What was he, exactly? "He's a friend's ex-boyfriend."

"This sounds like a domestic dispute. If you'd like to press charges or file a restraining order, you should go to your nearest precinct and file in person."

"I can't."

"Are you afraid for your life?"

"I just can't leave."

She cleared her throat. "Come again?"

"I don't leave my apartment."

There was a long pause. This was far more complicated than I'd imagined and I'd started to feel sick to my stomach. I considered hanging up.

"We can send an officer, but you'll have to give your name and address." I'd called the anonymous line for the precise reason that it was anonymous. Now, the only way to do anything was to allow the police to come here. That would mean another stranger, another situation I wanted no part of. And what if all this just made Lee angrier than he already was? People violated restraining orders all the time. A piece of paper couldn't protect me. I should've known they couldn't help. I learned that five years ago.

"No thank you," I said, and I hung up the phone.

I didn't tell Happy. And this isn't something the doctor needs to hear about now. I'll aim for a redirect. "How's the family?"

"Are you ready to be in this kind of situation?" He's referring to everything—all of it. And he might be making a solid point. How would I even know? I'm so full of fear, I've never been ready for anything. He looks at me like he sees right into my head and knows there are things I'm not telling him. "You haven't told me how you got the black eye."

I blow some air through my mouth, shrug my shoulders. "What are you suggesting?"

He puts a closed fist to his lips and clears his throat. "I'm not suggesting anything. I'm asking."

"This is ridiculous." I need to walk out the pins pricking my legs. I start to pace.

"Are you sleeping with her?" He leans forward. "Because if this is about sex, Wesley, there are other ways. I know it must get lonely, but—"

He doesn't even begin to understand. There is no sex. His bringing it up only further highlights my failure. Besides, what is he saying about her? "She's not a prostitute, you—"

The key turns in the lock. She's back.

"Christ, wait until you hear about the day I've had." She has her back turned as she comes in and flops her purse on the island, before moving to hang her coat on the rack. When she turns around and sees the Doctor, her chest heaves in surprise. "I didn't realize you had company, Wes."

"It happens." I send him an unpleasant look. I won't tell her that a moment ago, he all but called her a whore. That wouldn't be a proper introduction.

I hang her purse on the coat rack. As I pass her, she stops me by wrapping her thin fingers in the folds of my shirt and gives me a quick peck on the cheek. My skin tingles, just like it does anytime she touches me. It's a strange feeling somewhere between pleasant and unnerving because the contact excites me but I have to ask myself questions like did she put on that pomegranate ChapStick first? I tried to tell her that putting it in the fridge can kill the bacteria but she said it ruined the feel of it. In the living room, she stands before the Doctor, who's risen from his spot on the recliner. He watches her with an expressionless face.

"You must be Dr. Kidman."

"Charles, please." He shakes her hand. "And you must be Happy."

She smiles. "Wesley's told me a lot about you."

He looks at her, waits to speak a second longer than is appropriate for amicable conversation. "Wesley's told me a lot less about you."

How am I supposed to intercede? My heart swells, pushes against my chest, as I wait for Happy to react.

She laughs. "He's not always the most forthcoming."

The Doctor's shoulders droop. "Never has been."

Happy bites her lip. "Should we all sit down?" Her hospitality in my apartment is always impeccable. When the Doctor looks at me and raises an eyebrow, a wave of realization washes over Happy's features, and she adds, "Or am I interrupting?"

"Wesley?" The Doctor wants to know if I can stand to have him around a few minutes longer. No, he's trying to be considerate. I should respect that. I sit down.

Happy takes command of the conversation, never letting the silence simmer for too long. "I understand you know Wes's dad?"

"We're old friends." Dr. Kidman loves stories. As a clinical researcher, he spends all day, every day, listening to adult and juvenile depressives in varying degrees of study give accounts of their sad lives. Happy's doing him the ultimate service, letting him do the talking. She's a master at forcing people to like her. "We met at UC Berkeley back in `68. I was studying Psychology and Tom was studying Rhetoric. Berkeley was at the height of the peace movement—exciting times."

I've heard all of this before but I watch Happy, curious to see how she reacts to the story for the first time. She listens with an exaggerated expression of interest.

"I jumped right into graduate school. Tom spent a few years working for various civil rights organizations—did a couple of campaigns in San Francisco. When he decided it was time to grow up, he moved out to Denver for law school."

Happy's face lights up. She glances over at me and grins. I guess I hadn't ever told her that.

The Doctor sighs. "I'd never been to Colorado until I came out for Tom and Marjene's wedding, but I fell in love. I think it was the mountains."

Happy nods in agreement. There are so few Colorado natives. Everybody transplants for the Rocky Mountains. Are they really that impressive?

"I finished my PhD and continued working in California, teaching and publishing for a few years. Then, we came out here."

When he finishes, she beams. "I hope to study at DU."

He makes a humming noise, a little like a kazoo. All this academic talk gets the doctor excited. "In what field?"

"Art History."

"Another art enthusiast." He nods, glancing over at me. He's always been supportive of my career. "Wonderful. Are you an artist as well?"

"Not like Wes." She smiles, first at me and then at him. "I love textiles. Quilting mostly."

"We're very supportive of arts education." Now he has an opening to talk about his family. "I have an 8th grader at the Denver School of the Arts, and my youngest is a 4th grader at Bromwell."

I clear my throat. "He has daughters out of college too."

"My oldest is the same age as Wesley." He motions toward me. "I have another one who's 27. They both live in California. They're closer to my ex-wife."

I spent a good portion of the first 10 years of my life playing with the Doctor's daughters, but then the Doctor's marriage ended, like 50% of marriages do, and they went home to California with their mother. They used to come back here once a year for Christmas, but it's been ages since I've seen either of them. Dr. Kidman and Linda, who's 15 years younger, have been married for 15 years. She was his intern. Now, he's the parent of girls not too many years older than his first granddaughter. It's complicated.

Happy nods. "It sounds like you have a beautiful family." She won't pry. She'll wait until he leaves and then she'll get the whole story in a less direct, though more polite manner, by asking me.

"I do." He smiles. Then, he looks at his watch. He's done this fewer times since Happy arrived than I ever remember when he's talking to me. "Which reminds me, I should get going. I'll be late for dinner."

He stands. This is coming to an end. Just as I think I can take a deep breath, relax a little, Happy's expression is engulfed by an oversized grin, as though she's just been plugged into an electrical outlet.

"Hey, I have a crazy idea." She rises in pursuit of the Doctor. "What do you say to dinner? Here?" She looks at Dr. Kidman, and only Dr. Kidman, careful to avoid me as she speaks.

Has she lost her mind? I feel the heat creep up into my cheeks as my forehead begins to perspire.

"I'd love to meet your wife. And Wes's folks." Happy moves into the entryway and gets the Doctor's coat.

She doesn't need to do this. He can get his own coat. Besides, if anyone should be doing the hospitable thing, it should be me. This is my apartment. But I'm still standing in the living room, frozen at the words 'dinner' and 'here.'

She hands the Doctor his jacket. "It'd be a nice way for all of us to come together—get to know each other. Maybe this weekend?"

What the hell is she talking about? I wipe my forehead with the back of my hand and take a deep breath. Right now, it's only a suggestion, nothing that can't be squashed like a spider in the shower as soon as Dr. Kidman leaves.

He smiles as he pulls on his coat. "Sounds great." He looks at me. I look at the floor.

"We'll call you." She opens the door and sees him out. Then, she closes and locks up as though all of this is the most ordinary thing in the world. I can handle her referring to us as *we* and playing house. A certain change in the routine, the daily curveball I'm starting to catch with some frequency, but this?

I cross my arms, try to blink away the white splotches. "A dinner party?"

She leans against the door and scrunches her nose like a rabbit. "Why not?"

I laugh, slap my leg to emphasize the senselessness of it. "I can think of several hundred reasons."

"You can invite Rick." She takes a few, quick steps across the room. Now she thinks she's a cat. She stands in front of me, her arms around my neck, forehead pressed against mine. "It'll be fun."

"No." I cross my arms. There's nothing fun about any group of people invading my apartment, especially a group consisting of my parents, Dr. Kidman and Rick. It couldn't be less fun.

"Come on," she says. "I want to meet your family."

"No."

"Please?"

"I haven't met your dad either." I have thought about that, if and how I should.

"Come on, Wes. That's not fair." She puts her hands on her hips. "You know you can't until I figure everything out. There'd be too many questions."

"No," I say again. I'm starting to get lightheaded with this arguing.

"I'm serious, Wes. This is what normal people do."

The word "normal" is meant to cut us both. Neither one of us can say we've ever been in a relationship that could be classified as even close to normal. She's trying to prove something to herself as much as she is to me. Still, she can't possibly think this is a good idea. Then again, she doesn't really know. She hasn't seen them all together. She hasn't seen them here. But I look at her face and I can see it in her eyes. She wants this. What's more, as I kiss the tip of her nose, I want to give it to her. I'd ask myself, "What's the worst that could happen," but I don't think I want to know.

Chapter 14

I'm staring at the dinner table in my apartment—set for Happy and myself, and my parents, and Rick and his date, and the Doctor and his wife—and all I can think of is an old installation in the Brooklyn Museum I remember from Art History class: "The Dinner Party" by Judy Chicago. It's a flurry of porcelain and textile, where a sizable triangular table is set with thirty-nine settings to honor important women throughout history. Each place setting at the table has an artful, hand-sewn table runner (Happy's probably fond of this), golden chalice, and utensils. Then, designed with the individual time period of each woman in mind, the table is set with china-painted porcelain platters, standard dinner plate-sized representations of something that is a cross between a butterfly and a vulva. 39 of them stare up at you as you walk by, no mystery that you're looking at what you think you're looking at.

Imagine my horror as our professor at the time, hand-made jewelry and broomstick skirt- wearing woman, flashed each plate on slides for an entire week of class discussion, from the geometric curves of the Hatshepsut plate to the lacy, pink folds of Emily Dickinson. I remember this because it was one of the most unnerving experiences of my life. So here I am, because Happy thought this dinner party was a good idea and I went along with it. Now we're all at the table, and all I can think about is vulva-shaped plates as I stare down at the lasagna Happy baked in my kitchen, served in my dishes with my spatula. The twisting in my gut, like a tourniquet, suggests this dinner party will turn out a lot like that one.

My parents are seated beside one another on one side of the table, and Dr. Kidman and his wife are seated along the other. I'm sitting at one end, with Happy diagonally to my right. Rick sits at the other end with his date. A great deal of preemptive thought was put into how to best keep all the happy couples together.

While she organized the table, placed the settings, lit the candles, and cooked the food, I sat on the couch with my arms crossed and made a detailed mental list of all the ways in which this could end in catastrophe. There's a reason my parents and I only speak on the phone a few times a week at most. My mother comes once or twice every month. My father every few. Holidays are a disaster. Someone gets angry. My father and I butt heads. My mother weeps. End of story. It's never been easy for my mother to see me like this, for my father to admit to himself he has a son like me. My being here is an insult to the sacrifices they've both made on my behalf. Neither ever voices these regrets, at least not in a direct away, but it bubbles beneath the surface of every conversation, every expression of hope and subsequent disappointment, that I have remained here — the same.

This is not the only complication. My father's not fond of

Rick—an "enabler," he called him once. Nor is it likely that either my mother or Linda Kidman will approve of Rick's date. Then, there is the issue of Happy. They all want to know what she's doing here, what kind of funny business is going on. Am I paying her? Is she paying me in any number of ways? It can't be real, you see. I don't do real.

I knew this was on my parents' minds the moment they walked in the door. My mother gave Happy a forced smile, like someone had stuck a finger in each corner of her mouth and stretched. My father furrowed his eyebrows, like caterpillars, in her direction. Dr. Kidman was congenial, but his sphincter of a wife, whose face always looks a little sour, gave Happy a frigid handshake. I actually wished Rick would show up. That is until he did, as noisy as ever, clapping my father on the back, and telling my mother she was "looking good." His date, a pretty brunette named Jillian, hasn't spoken much. This may be a compliment to her common sense.

Now Happy's dishing dinner. She's in the zone, the perfect hostess, either ignorant of the hostility that fills the air with a sticky heat, or she's convinced that in good time, she's going to win them over.

"Good grub, Hapster," Rick says, as she hands him his plate with a heaping slice. It's some kind of fancy lasagna, with layers of spinach, and several types of cheese. The sauce is tomato-based. I look at the mammoth serving on Rick's plate and I can already feel it sitting heavy in my gut. I don't know if I can do this.

"It does look delicious." My mother tries.

"Thank you." Happy floats like a dandelion seed above the

tension that has arisen around her presence. She bubbles at the compliment, floats a smile in my direction. "It was my mother's recipe. She called it 'Cupid Lasagna,' because it tastes so good you'll fall in love."

"That's cute," Jillian says. It's nice to know the only one whose first impression isn't going to exacerbate the unease of this situation finds Happy amusing.

Happy lifts her fork and goes in for a chunk of her slice. "Dig in, everyone."

The entire table follows suit and a moment later mouths chew up and down amidst a cacophony of swallowing. Something inexplicable happens. Almost as soon as pasta hits taste buds, shoulders slacken, tightened faces begin to loosen, and expressions soften. Every person in the room humanizes. People smile, converse even. Dr. Kidman asks my father about work and he jumps on the opportunity. He spins a yarn about his current class action against a fast food chain that doesn't make all its locations wheelchair accessible. He gets all riled up, and Happy nods along, feigning active engagement, espousing her own opinions on civil liberties, winning them over on points of politics. This conversation sustains us through much of dinner. Then, I pour myself another glass of wine. I'm breaking my rules again, but it's that kind of a night. The warmth of it relaxes me a little.

"What's for dessert?" Rick asks, running his finger along his plate, sopping up the last bit of sauce from his third helping. You can always leave it to Rick to dash any hope of leftovers. He licks his fingers, producing a loud smacking noise that makes me cringe.

The garlic toast is almost gone too. Even the Caesar salad has been disposed of.

Happy looks at Rick. "Linda was kind enough to make something."

"Come on, Rick." Jillian's on her feet. "Let's clear these plates."

"Thanks." Happy gives them both a kind nod. This woman seems awfully well-mannered to be on a dinner date with Rick.

"Help me with the dessert, Marjene?" Linda sounds conspiratorial. My mother looks at her and nods, and the two move toward the kitchen. They have much to discuss, I'm sure. My mother's taken Linda on as a sort of apprentice over the years, a younger wife to train. It gives her a place to exert her efforts now that she doesn't see me so often. My mother was always fussing about something growing up—every cough was pertussis and every stomachache was appendicitis. I spent hours in the emergency room. While these trips never amounted to any sort of dire diagnosis, I suppose they put the idea in my head that my body was always working against me, that some disease or ailment always lurked, ready to take me down. But it would be unjust to blame this all on her. These kinds of things are never that straightforward. Now she gets unexplained headaches on an almost daily basis. She's started seeing an acupuncturist but he can't seem to help her either. No one ever can.

All this movement leaves me at the table with my father and Dr. Kidman. My muscles tense. Happy reaches out and takes my hand.

"Charlie tells me you're thinking of doing your Master's at

DU?" My father turns his attention to Happy. "In art?"

Happy smiles. "Art History."

"Very interesting." My father speaks in layers. On the surface, he sounds like he's just making conversation. He picks up his wine glass without making eye contact and swirls it in his hand. He lifts it to his nose, smells it, and then takes a sip. He's on his fourth. "A tough business though, I'd imagine."

Happy opens her mouth to answer but my father continues. It's a game he plays, in which he continues with veiled accusations, but doesn't leave time for a response. In the courtroom, it's a rhetorical strategy. I think they call it leading the witness. "Wesley's always been like that," he says. "Obviously you know. I bet you like that painting." He bobs his head in the direction of the Kandinsky. He always brings this up, as if his opinion on my wall art means anything to anyone. He has an antique world map hanging in his study. The frame cost more than the print itself. I could remind him that I have a shelf full of my successful work, but it wouldn't help. At the end of the day, my faults are a failure of his parenting. Every time he sees me, he's reminded of that. But none of that matters now. This is about Happy.

"I don't mind it." Happy smiles. "It's a little frantic." She squeezes my hand. "As for the business, I'd like to be the one who facilitates the way people experience art and how that experience will be conveyed."

If *that* wasn't an answer. My father's not sure what to say. Dr. Kidman chuckles. If it didn't have to be in front of everyone, I'd lean over and kiss Happy on the cheek.

"Are we ready?" Linda's voice echoes from the kitchen.

"Yes, please." Rick rubs his belly. Rick and Jillian have been at the sink. It looks like they've taken to starting the dishes. That must have been her idea. Rick's style of washing dishes is like taking a military shower on Pfaltzgraff.

"What're we having?" I ask, because someone should.

Linda beams. She must think it's a real treat. "Hope you like apple pie."

The two older women have already plated each slice and carry the dessert plates over, placing one in front of each guest with an accompanying dessert fork. They serve their husbands first, then Rick and his date, followed by Happy and myself, and they each sit down with their own small pieces. They're showing us how it's done.

Happy smiles when the plate is set before her. "This looks great."

The pie crust is a little doughy but it's good. We're all enjoying it, except for Linda, who just picks hers apart, holding her fork in her bony hand, as though she's digging for hidden treasure in the middle. I'm about to ask why she would bake something she doesn't even eat, but I see the way Dr. Kidman is scraping his empty plate, careful to mop up every last bit, and I think I understand. I enjoy the first half of my pie in temperate peace, listening to Rick talk about how he and Jillian met at the Art Institute, where Rick teaches. Jillian is a financial aid advisor — a serious woman with a serious profession. An oddity.

Then, my father pushes his plate away. "What do you do now, Happy?" "I've been working at my father's store but — "

"Delivering groceries." My father takes a drink of his wine. He knows damn well this is how we met.

"If you think you already know the answers, why are you asking questions?" I say.

Happy ignores us both. "I help with some of the administrative portion of running the store; overseeing deliveries, bookkeeping, that kind of thing. But, I've just started a second job at a craft store. I'm going to start teaching a quilting class."

"Is that hourly?" he takes another sip of wine. "Must make it difficult to pay rent."

"Happy'll be a great teacher. People really get off on hearing her speak." It's the most inappropriate thing I could have said. I should have never refilled my wine. Happy stares at me with narrow eyes as red spreads across the pale skin of her cheeks.

My father looks from me to Happy, then back to me. "I'm not sure what you mean, son."

Happy kicks me under the table at the same time as she clears her throat. "I'm not either."

"Nothing." I reach for my water glass. "Just a joke. Wasn't funny."

"I don't think any of this is a joke." His tone's changed again. This is the Judy Chicago nightmare; the vulva china is coming down with a crash. "Here you are, a 33 year old shut-in who can't even take care of himself, and now you've got a squatter."

Dr. Kidman looks from him to me, caught between the father and his son.

"All finished?" Happy's on her feet, collecting the dessert plates at lightning speed. She disappears into the kitchen.

My father continues. "We're all sitting around, having dinner, pretending everything's normal. Nothing is normal. This —" he motions around the apartment, "isn't normal. That —" he points to Happy, who has her back turned in the kitchen, "isn't normal. He —" he points at me "isn't God damned normal. I'm sick of pretending any of this is *ever* going to be normal."

"Tom please." My mother puts her hand on his forearm. Her fingers are thin and frail, knotted, like the skeletal branches of an aspen tree. I look at Dr. Kidman, waiting for him to jump in, say something in my defense, but he just looks down at his plate. He won't interfere.

"What is normal, really?" Linda muses. A standard response from the wife of a shrink.

Rick rearranges the phlegm in the back of his throat. "This pie was sure tasty." Poor Rick. He's about as confrontational as my coat rack.

Happy's rinsing the dessert plates. Her arms move in a quick, circular motion, like the blades of a fan, with the sponge clenched in her tight fist. I'm so busy watching Happy, I'm not paying attention to the fact that every other pair of eyes in the room has settled on me. They all stare, waiting to see how I'll react. Will I take my father's challenge? Lock horns with the bull elk? Or will I play the part of the subservient son?

I let my eyes settle on the table cloth. It's a rich burgundy with a satin striped pattern. A little festive for November, but the only one large enough to fit the table once the leaf was added. I run my hand along the edge, smoothing out a wrinkle in front of where I sit. My stomach twists in knots and I think about excusing myself.

But this is my space and I have to take control. For Happy and for me. I take a deep breath and I raise my head.

I look at my father. "Get out."

"What?" His eyes are wide.

"I said 'out.' Everybody. Dinner is over." I push my chair back and rise from the table.

I move slow and deliberate, so that I appear calm, but firm, as I make for the coat rack. Rick and his date hop up as though they're being timed. Dr. Kidman stands slowly. He looks at me from over the rim of his glasses as he has so many times before and I know he's trying to tell me he's sorry about all of this. That doesn't matter now. Linda also stands. When my mother gets to her feet, my father reaches out and grabs her. She settles back into her chair.

He leans back and folds his arms across his chest. "You would kick your own parents to the curb?"

I've seen this face before. I remember it clearly. My father had arranged to take time off to drive us to a traveling carnival that had set up in the parking lot of a Catholic Church. The forecast called for wind. My mother worried this made the rides unsafe, might pose an even larger threat than the risk she'd already taken by accepting the proposal in the first place. They'd argued. Finally my father looked at me watching from just outside the kitchen and asked, "What about you, son?"

I looked to my mother for a moment as she shook her head. Then my father, eyes narrowing, like he already knew what the answer would be. Mother had spoken of danger, always afraid of Colorado's unpredictable weather.

"No," I said, looking at her and not him. He sighed and I blinked to find his gaze had constricted, as though the skin of his forehead was being pulled downward by some invisible force. I see these eyes when he looks at me now, eyes that can't believe I've gone and let him down again. I turn my head toward the entryway, focus on another part of this small room.

Rick and Jillian already have their coats. Rick teeters at the door. He desperately wants to leave, but doesn't know what to say. Jillian pops into the kitchen to whisper something to Happy. She puts a hand on her shoulder, gives it a squeeze. Dr. Kidman helps Linda into her coat.

I motion out the window in the living room. "I hear the view by the river is nice."

"You stubborn—"

"Well, thanks for dinner." Rick's voice booms over everyone. "I'll call you later." I walk them out. At the door, Rick whispers, "Good luck," and smacks me on the arm. I give him a nod as he ushers Jillian down the hall. She seems nice. I could stand to meet her again under better circumstances.

"Thanks for having us," Dr. Kidman says. He and his wife are up next. "We need to get home, take care of the sitter." They all seem to have forgotten that I've kicked them out. But, if this makes him feel better about the whole thing, as though there hasn't been a betrayal, let him have his congenial farewell.

Happy's emerged from the kitchen. The skin around her eyes looks swollen and her cheeks are splotched with red. She blots at her eyes, looking down at her feet as though she's the one who should feel ashamed. This is unacceptable. I clench my fists and bite back the urge to scream. She shakes Dr. Kidman's hand and thanks Linda for the pie.

I touch Dr. Kidman's arm at the door. "Thanks for your help."

He looks at me, opens his mouth like he might say something. But he doesn't. He just shakes his head and looks down at his feet. Then they're out the door and down the hall and out of my hair. Now, just my parents remain.

"Out." I reiterate my previous sentiment. I want him gone. I always want him to leave, watch the seconds tick by as he inspects the apartment, calls out every little action that reminds us both that I'm not the son he thought he'd have. I feel a strange exhilaration in finally saying this out loud.

"Wesley, please." My mother gets to her feet, ignoring my father's grabbing hands. She pleads with watery eyes. This conflict makes her heart beat faster, her head spin. She's begging me to let her have her peace. But she can't stop the worrying—never could.

I will not bend to her sad face—the dazed expression, the hand to her chest. I want them out of here. I cross my arms and look away. She sighs with a tragic, high-pitched moan, almost inaudible through the exhalation, and moves to the coat rack. She's relented. She buttons up and throws her purse over her shoulder. "I know when we aren't welcome. Come on, Tom."

My father stands. "To be so mistreated by my own child," he says as he passes me and moves for his own coat. "After everything I've done."

He buttons the first button with such violence he might pop it right off. When he realizes he hasn't lined the holes up, he lets out a throaty growl, unbuttons and does it over again. I stand, arms crossed, without a word. I'll not engage either of them further, because that's what they want. My silence will pain them most.

Happy looks at me, sucks on her bottom lip. She keeps her head down but looks up with eyebrows arched, like a teenager rethinking an insult slung at an ill-deserving peer. "Nice meeting you both." She doesn't owe him this courtesy.

This is the final straw. My father laughs, shakes his head. Then, with a hand on my mother's back, guiding her along as he's always felt the need to do, he pushes her out the door. I close the door behind them and make sure everything is locked. It's over now.

"That was awful." Happy sniffs as she speaks. Her eyes brim with tears, like a water glass dangerously over-filled.

I want to say the right thing, but I just don't know how. "This dinner was your idea."

She starts to cry. For real. Tears and sobs—a great noise. I come to her, but I pause. Does she want me to touch her, to hold her? Or does she want to be left alone?

She moves closer to me, buries her face against my shoulder. She wraps her thin arms around me. Now I know. I hold her. I put my chin against the top of her head, lean down and kiss her hair. The tropical smell of her shampoo still lingers, even this late into the day. The thought makes me want to keep kissing her, to get over my own fears and make her feel better, but I can't ignore my utter inadequacy. I couldn't even shield her from my own family. I will not add to her disappointment by trying and failing again. I take a step back and put my hands at my side.

She looks up at me. She still has tears in her eyes, but she smiles a half smile. "Let's not do that again."

Chapter 15

It's finally snowed—not heavy. We still haven't had a generous snowfall in the Denver metro area. But it has snowed—light dustings. It's the first of December and at last it feels like winter. In the morning when I wake up, my body aches with the stiffness of the previous night's freeze. Happy's taken to sleeping in one of my long sleeved t-shirts. Despite the implications of sharing a bed, the longing we both feel but don't verbalize because I can't bring myself to act on it and she doesn't want to make it worse, her bare legs are warm against me. Her feet are ice cold. She refuses to sleep in socks. I've added an extra blanket, folded at the bottom.

Everything's cooling down. Something's shifted in the initial surprise that was Happy's being here. In the days since our dinner party, a chill has filled the corners of the apartment, the empty spaces. Sometimes I don't notice it. There are moments, many moments, when we smile. Happy laughs. We continue to explore the newness of all of this, of each other. But there's still a wall between us, one we hack away at, but that hasn't come down completely. I'm not ready.

Happy is gluttonous for information. She wants to know

everything about my past, my present, my hopes and dreams. She wants to know where I've been and where I want to be. These are not easy questions for me to answer but in the quiet of a late night in my bedroom, with our faces pressed so close together I can feel her warm breath on my skin, I try to answer as best I can. I try to tell her that, as hard as it is to believe, there are things that matter. I have goals. I will always have a desire to create. It's easier not to tell her this life is so different than the one I thought I'd have, the one I continue to miss out on every day that I stay in my apartment. I've learned to tread lightly on the hypotheticals.

I'm afraid to know half as much about Happy, but she wants to tell me, and I listen because I like to watch her as she talks, to hear her voice, the way her body moves as she tells her stories. I listen to her talk about the way her summer trip to Europe turned into a year-long residency, how she met a man and she stayed long enough for him to break her heart and then she came home. She's been picking up the pieces ever since, finishing school and trying to understand what it means to grow up, but she keeps finding herself in the same situations over and over again. I listen to all her secrets — the parts of her heart she locks in a box, like the one I keep in the kitchen. I listen to the things she doesn't say, the thoughts that whisper behind her words, how it's always her fault in the end. This is how I've come to know her. It's a different kind of intimacy. One I'm not used to because I haven't ever shared my life, and Happy isn't used to because for her, this part, if it comes at all, comes after sex.

Other times, the chill that lives in nooks and crannies creeps up along the wall and across the ceiling and it grips us. We bicker more than any two people in an enclosed space should. Sometimes it's about the little things, like where Happy should keep her toothbrush or why it's important to use bleach to scrub the bathtub. Sometimes, we compromise. Other times, one or the both of us is unwilling to bend. So we try to move on because we both know how easily the other could break. Sometimes, we fight about things that can't be fixed. We fight about how I told Dr. Kidman not to bother to stop by anymore. I'm not ready to forgive him yet. We fight about Thanksgiving because I'm not talking to my parents and Happy wants to spend the holiday with her father but she doesn't want me to be alone. This is hard. This is when I catch her with that hazy look in her eyes. She wonders what she's doing here. If this can ever be something that will last.

It's times like this when I think maybe I could just go. Maybe I could walk out the door and get in her car and bring her father a bottle of wine, hand it to him when we arrive on his doorstep. But I can't leave, not for turkey or pumpkin pie and not to meet Happy's dad and I can't bear the thought of letting her see me fail. Sometimes it's better not to try. So she has Thanksgiving with her dad and brings me a plate of leftovers. We sit on the couch while I eat microwaved turkey and gravy, stuffing, yams, and cranberry sauce. When she goes into the kitchen to cut us two slices of pumpkin pie, she reaches into the fridge and pulls out a can of whipped cream.

"What is that?"

"I know you don't do dairy, but it's pumpkin pie."

"I'd never eat it out of a can." Not to mention the fact that aerosol cans are incredibly harmful to the ozone layer.

"Come on," she says and then squirts a little in her mouth.

The sound of it is like I'm in a wind tunnel. Her mouth has touched the nozzle. She brought it from her father's house. Did he do the same thing? Is it a fresh can? And, where's the cap? It shouldn't sit in the refrigerator unprotected like that. The thought of all the bacteria growing on the nozzle, let alone inside the can itself, makes me sick. "Please stop."

She puts the can on the counter and looks at me. "Okay. No whipped cream."

She throws the can in the trash and we eat our pumpkin pie and watch "A Charlie Brown Thanksgiving" until my cell buzzes. Happy pauses the DVR.

"Who is it?"

"My mother."

"Are you going to answer it?"

"No."

"It's a holiday." She puts her hand on my thigh, gives it a squeeze.

I sigh, then click the green button. "Hello?"

"Wesley, it's so good to hear your voice. I've been so worried about you."

"We're watching a movie." I put my arm around Happy.

"Oh, you are." She doesn't say anything for a few seconds. "Well, I won't bother you then. Just wanted to say Happy Thanksgiving and I love you. Your father too."

"Okay." I say and then hang up.

"How's your mom?" Happy lifts her head up from my chest and looks at me.

"Same as always." She looks poised to respond but I cut her off. "Let's just watch, okay?"

She lays her head back against my chest and presses play. As we sit on the couch I feel the chill recede. All I can do is wait here until something brings it out again.

Something's been wrong for a while. Happy's upset or sad, unhappy or tired. I'm not sure. And I want to ask her but I can't, because if I do, I'm afraid she'll realize she has no reason to stay. After all, what's she doing here with me in the first place? We can't go on like this forever. We can only go for so long until she needs me to leave with her, for some reason, large or small, and I won't be able to do it.

It's the end of this particular day; the sky's black and Happy's late. I've already heated myself some leftovers for dinner because I was hungry and she wasn't here and I couldn't wait. She had a shift at the craft store this afternoon and sometimes she gets food with a coworker. But she's gotten lazy about calling or texting, letting me know what her plans are. She says she forgets. I've been worrying. I haven't been able to hold a pen long enough to ink a single line. I resent her rendering me unproductive. When I hear the key turn in the door, I race to unlock the chain.

"Where have you been?" I cross my arms as she pushes past me.

She hates when I lock up knowing she'll be coming, but it's after 9:00 pm on a Thursday and she's been gone since late morning and the key turning in the door is the first I have heard from her. I have to keep myself protected.

"Out." She puts her purse on the kitchen in the island, in the same place she always puts it, and I move it to the coat rack.

"Out where?"

I know she gets off around 5:00 pm. Even if she grabbed a bite somewhere near the craft store, I can't imagine it could take four hours to make it back here. I don't keep a schedule. Not really. I have deadlines, and I adhere to them with a steady sense of purpose, but when there's never any need to go out, to get from one point to another, schedules are simple. Business is all about location, and Happy has several of those. She goes from the grocery store to the craft store to wherever else, in any combination, on a daily basis. I hate that I know all of this.

Her body tenses and she moves with the spirit of someone who's caught wind of a nasty rumor and has waited all day to confront the culprit — like Scout Finch and Walter Cunningham. He took quite a beating. The entire apartment resonates with nervous energy. The hair stands on my arms. The chill creeps in from underneath the door. "Does it matter?"

She has a point there. I wouldn't really appreciate anything she did out there anyway. Why does it matter? Why does it bother me so much that she doesn't want to tell me?

"I'm sorry." She sighs and plops down on the couch. Then, she waves for me to come and join her. I move across the room and sit down beside her, and she lies down so that her head is in my lap. Perhaps it's not so cold after all.

I reach out and stroke her hair with the tips of my fingers

and the way her head leans into my touch suggests that I'm doing the right thing. Her entire body relaxes against the couch. The room unwinds and I close my eyes and take a deep breath. For a moment, everything feels natural. But her body tenses just as quickly as it settled and she sits up and looks at me.

"Why can't I put my purse on the counter?"

I blink. "What?"

"Why do you always move it?"

The obvious answer is the germs. Some studies show that women's handbags carry more bacteria than toilets. And I'm afraid it will get knocked off the counter and spill, create a mess or a dangerous situation if someone were to trip and fall. And it's important for me to decide where things go when they are in my space, that it can't always be up to her, but don't know how to say any of this in a way that sounds rational. So I don't say anything.

"Why can't it be on the counter, if I want it on the counter?" She jumps off the couch and starts pacing the living room.

"I don't understand—"

"Of course you don't." She shakes her head. "You never understand anything potentially hazardous to your delicate system." This isn't the first time we've addressed my process, but this is the first time her resentment burns.

I stumble for an answer. "I—"

"I should be able to be gone all day if I want to be and not get the third degree when I walk in the door, you know?" She puts her hands on her hips and stands over me.

This makes my skin twinge. I push into the couch away

from her.

"I'm not like you, Wes. I need to get out. I need to be out. I need to see people, meet people. God, I just need to do something."

"I understand." This seems like the right thing to say. This is what we're all supposed to need.

"No, you don't." She waves her arms. "That's the problem. You don't understand because you don't want to. I thought, maybe if I— if we—that things would be different. But, they're not. I'm not sure they ever will be." She takes a step back, looks down at the floor. "I don't want to be your caretaker. I can't be a caretaker. Not again."

I fold my hands in my lap. "I never said this would be easy."

She sighs. "Of course not." She moves back over to the couch, sits down on the other end, turning to face me. "You've made it clear how difficult you are. How crazy you are. There's no mistaking that." She puts her head in her hands, runs her fingers through her hair. I can see by the way her actions are weighted, like every little motion is moving a mountain, that she's been wrestling with this for some time. "I'm not sure I can do this. I have to fight you, to push you, on every single thing we do. Aren't you exhausted too? I thought I could help you, but maybe this whole thing is bad for the both of us." She takes a step backward and folds in on herself, crossing her arms so that her chest caves in a little. "You can't even bring yourself to sleep with me. What does that mean?"

The cold is back. It's settled into the apartment like a dense cloud, and something about the way it clings to my body, makes the tiny bumps raise on my skin, suggests that this time it's here to stay. I want to get up and adjust the thermostat, put some hot water on for tea, anything to fight it. But now is not the time. I think about reaching out and taking her hand, comforting her. But that's part of the problem. She hasn't felt me enough. I've made her think I don't want to feel her.

"What do you have to say?" she asks.

What do I have to say? I want to tell her that I want her here, that she should stay. I want to tell her that I care for her. I want to tell her that I want to be with her, that I'm trying to be. I want to tell her those things, but I can't. I can't move. I can't breathe. My chest tightens and the cold takes over. Only a few seconds have passed, and yet I think we both know that she's been hoping for an instant answer. I just can't give her one.

"You can leave your key on the counter." The words sting as they exit my mouth, as I've been holding an ice cube on my tongue. Her face falls, every muscle relaxing into a moment of despair, and then acceptance. If I could take them back, I would. But the words have already poisoned the space like noxious gas, burning my eyes and nose.

She doesn't speak. Instead, she moves to the counter and slams down her key. Then, she turns and goes into the bedroom. Has she already packed? Did she know we'd have this conversation today? That it would end this way? I rise from my chair and move to the counter, picking up the key. It's still warm from being wrapped in her clenched fist, as though it were a butterfly that might flit away if she were to give it the chance.

As she returns to the living room with her awful suitcase,

I know it's too late. She's planned an exit strategy for a while. She gets her other suitcase, the smaller one that stacks on top, out of the closet in the hall. Then she pops into the bathroom and returns with her tote. I look at her bags. This always felt temporary. She rolls her way into the living room without a word, collects her coat and her purse, careful not to look at me, and slips out the front. She slams the door behind her without another word and I know. I've ruined this. Just like I knew I would.

Later that night, after I've thrown away the dinner I can't bring myself to eat, I lay alone in my bed for a few hours, staring at the crack in the ceiling. I can just barely see it in the moonlight. I can't fall asleep. I can't stop thinking about all the things I should have said to her, how if I was just a little bit better at thinking on my feet, I could have asked her to stay. Maybe she would have. Maybe she'd be here in bed beside me right now. But I know this isn't true. This is about so much more than what I did or did not say. This is about what I won't do, what I can't. We could have sex. I could try harder to let that happen. Still, even at my best, how could I ever be enough for her? I can't even leave my apartment. That's what she needs. She needs someone who can go after her. Who cares enough to follow. What if I could care that much?

I get up and find my shoes at the foot of the bed. I don't have time to change my clothes. I bet she's gone to her father's house. I don't know where he lives but once I get out the door I can call her on the way. Once I get out, I can figure out how to get there.

I just need to get out. I grab my wallet and house key off the top of my dresser and head into the hall. I turn all the lights on in the apartment. I'll leave them on when I go. Now, here I am, standing in front of the open door. I stare out into the empty hall, dimly lit by soiled light fixtures. It's going to be cold out there. I should get a coat. This is crazy. I'm wearing my pajamas and I didn't even put socks on. I don't even know where I'm going. And I forgot to grab my phone. How can I call her if I don't have my phone? If I am going to do this, I need to think about it. I can't just go out there. Anything could happen. Anything.

Then, it starts. I feel the tightening in my chest as the light blazes up in white spots. My arms and legs slacken as my vision narrows and the hallway seems further away. It could be seconds, minutes, even longer. I don't know. The sweat beads on my forehead. My body's being crushed beneath a pile of bricks. If I don't close the door I'm going to black out. I lock up and slide to the floor. I put my head between my legs and try to blink away the pressure. My eyes fill with hot tears—they run down my cheeks. After a few moments have passed and the panic has subsided, I sit up and press my head to the door. Happy was right to leave.

Outside

Inside my apartment, nothing is the same. It's been a week, and I've put off my grocery order, living on restaurant deliveries and stale back pantry contents — a well-matched diet for the cold that still covers every surface. I haven't been able to bring myself to call *Lafferty's*. But this morning my hunger, not to mention my fear of monosodium glutamate, got the best of me and I called in an order. After all, MSG symptom complex was originally called the "Chinese Restaurant Syndrome" for a reason.

I stand in my kitchen, putting away the extra set of dishes still laid out on the rack by the sink. I've thought about them every time I've come into the kitchen for the past week. Every day, for three meals, a few snacks, and several refills of water, I've considered that I'll no longer need two of anything on a daily basis. It seems fitting, with my groceries coming just like they used to before her, that I should put them away today.

I've just opened my cabinet to return the plate, when the doorbell buzzes. The noise causes a jolt in my chest, as though I've just grabbed hold of an electric fence. I drop the plate. It crashes to the floor and splits, tiny triangular pieces of ceramic scattering across the linoleum, like I'm tiling mosaic in my kitchen. It's almost beautiful.

"Just a minute." I step around the mess, careful not to get any pieces caught in my shoe. I should clean it up, but the door waits to be opened, and I'm eager to see who's behind it.

When I called this morning to place my order, nothing felt amiss with Mr. Lafferty. He was courteous, told me someone would arrive later with the delivery. Someone. But not who I want it to be. I've played the events of the past several weeks over in my head, as though I've been locked in a room and tied down in front of the screen, forced to watch a repeating reel of my own subliminal video. Everything, each memory, sound, feeling, touch of skin, is trying to tell me something. Not that it matters. Epiphanies only bear meaning when you have the power to see them through. I don't have the power to do anything. I guess I can open my door.

I start to unlock, then pause at the top chain. This is it—the reset. A familiar weight seizes my sternum, as though my body is being buried in wet concrete. I lean against the door, struggle to hold myself up. I clench a fist around the doorknob and wait out this brief period of incapacity. When I can open the door, it's as if every ounce of energy, my very essence, has drained from my body. I am nothing but a fleshy shell.

Angel holds my groceries in his arms, same slicked back hair and professional attire as I remember. My regular grocery boy stands before me as he has so many times before, and I feel the weight of it, like the groans of a longstanding house resettling over time. I'm caught with glimpses of the old life colored with the innate knowledge that what comes next will never feel quite right. She's distorted it all. Not because she's made changes to my daily routine. She has, a great many. But because she herself was a change, an alteration to the interior world of my apartment, and I can't go back to the way it was before she was here.

"Come in." I point to the kitchen as though the young man has forgotten. Maybe he has. "How's your grandma?" I ask because it's the only thing left to say.

Chapter 1

It's an early Thursday morning, ten days since that day, and fifteen days before Christmas. I'm in the kitchen cleaning up the remnants of last night's dinner, because after Rick left in a huff at 1:00 in the morning, I was too tired to touch the mess. The fact that I could even get in a few hours of sleep before cleaning up this disaster should be some kind of accomplishment—too bad I'm the only one here to appreciate it. The smell of garlic and tomato sauce from the meatball subs we ate for dinner still stinks up the apartment. Six empty cans of Pabst Blue Ribbon sit on my counter, some of them caved in on themselves, arranged like a miniature collection of lopsided bowling pins. The beer makes a sorry substitute for Rick's usual high quality selections of Colorado brewers. It seems some trendsetters from God knows where decided it was hip to drink cheap beer out of cans and when Rick is the only one who can pick up dinner, I'm at his mercy.

We'd spent our night going over some of his preliminary color work. For the most part, this draft is solid, but we've got a late January deadline and we'd spent most of the night struggling over a particular set of frames.

"I just don't know what you want, man." Rick had pushed the printed pages across the table. "Night is night."

"It's more than that," I said. The frame at the center of our debate depicts the moment before the children are attacked by Bob Ewell. It's a dark night; the children can't see. But more than that, there's the tense notion of something coming. "It's the stillness before the thunderstorm."

"That's really great." Rick crushed a beer can in his hand. "And, what color is that?"

I wanted to tell him it's a sort of silver blue, a luminosity even the most expert colorist might struggle to replicate — paramount to that single frame. But I didn't understand why he'd gotten so frustrated. All I was asking was for him to do his job. "You're the colorist," I said instead.

"Nice." Rick set the beer can down on the table. "Look, maybe we should call it a night."

I couldn't let him give up. I jumped to my feet. "We're not finished. Not until you figure this out."

"Jesus, Wes. Relax." Rick put his hands out like he was trying to keep someone from starting a fist fight. "I'll have to think about it and come back to it."

"We need to do it now." My voice came out louder than I'd meant. But I didn't understand why he wouldn't help me get this done.

He shook his head. "We have some time, you know. This project's not going anywhere."

I crossed my arms. "Neither am I."

Rick paused, picked up his empty beer can and tapped the

table. Then, he said, "Who's fault is that?"

This abruptness shocked me. I took a step back. "What?"

"I'm sorry. That was out of line." Rick pushed back in his chair. "It's just… have you even called her?"

Why did it have to come to that? "She left," I said, picking up his beer can and taking it to the kitchen. I put it on the counter with the others. "That's it."

"You're right," he said, standing up. "Always."

"What's wrong with you?" I asked him.

"What's wrong with you?"

I opened my mouth to respond but he shook his head again. "Save it," he said. "I'm tired, you know? I'll talk to you tomorrow."

In the kitchen, I go to throw away the empty cans when I hear a faint hum coming from down the hall. My phone is vibrating. I'd plugged it into the charger on the nightstand when I collapsed into bed. I reach the bedroom just as the phone falls silent. I flip the light switch but teeter in the doorway. My mind leaps to the list of potential deaths the vibrating no doubt heralds. It's only a little after 6:00 AM. People rarely call me outside of standard operating hours—this can't be good. My father's had the inevitable heart attack after a lifetime spent devouring enough red meat to feed the entire state of Texas. My mother's wrecked her car on icy roads. My initial gut reaction would be that Rick has drunk himself to death, maybe taken a drug at some party, but if that were the case, who would be calling on his behalf and why would they be calling me? I'm not sure he even likes me right now.

How would I handle it if any of these scenarios were true?

How would I grieve alone in my sanctuary, unable to pay my respects in the traditional way? If Happy were still here, she'd have crawled across the right side of the bed and grabbed the phone before I even reached the doorway. I should at least see who's called. By staying here I can bite back the acrid taste of impending distress that makes my throat burn. I take one cautious step into the bedroom, caught halfway between in and out. I take a breath.

The phone buzzes a second time against the wooden nightstand. Now I have no choice but to answer. I grab the time bomb just as it stops vibrating and my stomach does a flip flop. The screen reads two missed calls. Happy.

Should I call her back? I can't imagine why she'd be calling so early in the morning. Why would she be calling at all? I glance down at the phone again and my mind floods with possible explanations. An accidental dial? I've seen the way she shoves her phone in the back pocket of her jeans. It would be easy enough to do. But she's called twice. Perhaps it's business related, something's happened at the grocery store and she's been the one tasked with notifying customers. I'm not the only person to get deliveries. Maybe she's realized she left something here and needs to pick it up. But I would have found it by now. Besides, it's too early in the morning for something so trivial. It has to be important. Angel? His grandmother? I hope not. Maybe something's wrong with her. A pressure pushes against my sternum like an expanding balloon. I move my thumb to redial when it buzzes again. The picture she took appears behind her name. She smiles at an upward angle, where she held the phone above her head against my pillow. I guess I forgot to delete it.

I press the green button. "Hello?"

"Wes?"

"Happy?" I ask, which is silly because I already know.

"God, I'm glad you answered." She lets out a constricted laugh.

"Is something wrong?" She isn't calling to tell me she misses me.

Her voice rasps in the receiver. "I don't know where to start." She pauses. "I need your help."

The disbelief sparks in my laugh. "My help?"

"I need you to call Rick and ask him to come pick me up."

Why Rick? I hadn't pictured him taking part in our hypothetical reunion. And why does she need a ride somewhere? "You have a car." At least she did the last time I saw her.

A heavy sigh echoes in the crackle of the connection. "This is an emergency. I need you to call Rick and tell him to come get me. I'm at The Dollhouse." So many things about this statement, her frantic tone, evade my logic. "I'm in a room downstairs and the door is locked. He'll have to find a key."

Why is she back there? Why is the door locked? None of this is making sense. The balloon in my chest inflates a little more. I scoot to the edge of the mattress, give myself a quick succession of taps on the cheek, the one that's not pressed against my phone. That refocuses the pain enough to ask a question. "What's going on?"

"Damn it, Wesley." Her voice is louder now. "I don't have time for this. He could be back any minute."

My mind snags on the rusty nail of 'he.' I don't know how I know, but I do. "Lee."

"It's not what you think."

"Doesn't matter."

Her laugh tells me we both know this isn't true. "Look. I'm alone in a dark room in the basement of this shitty club, the last place I'd ever thought I'd be again, and my battery is in the red and I'm pretty sure when Lee comes back he's going to hurt me. Could you please call Rick?"

"I should call the police."

"You can't." Her voice raises again and I pull the phone away from my ear. "Listen, Wes. There's some really bad shit happening here. Prostitution. Drugs. I don't know what else. But these girls, it's not their fault, you know? I promised I wouldn't call the cops until the girls had a chance to clear out. Some of them aren't even here legally. They're not the ones who deserve the trouble."

"Oh," I say. That's a lot of information. I'm not sure her logic is sound but before I can argue she starts talking again.

"Call Rick, okay? I'm going to call the cops. I want to be the one to do it. But, I've got to get out of here first." Her voice calms. "My phone's going to die but I'll tell you the whole story later."

"You will?" I run my foot across the floor. I hope I don't sound too hopeful.

"Just get Rick, okay? Tell him to go around to the service entrance in the back."

I nod. "Okay."

I'm thinking maybe the line's gone dead when she clears

her throat. "Hey, Wesley?" A timid whisper.

"Yeah?"

"Thanks."

"Okay."

I hang up. Then, I dial Rick's number. It rings and rings and he doesn't answer. I hang up and try again. He's always been a heavy sleeper, could sleep through multiple alarms when we were in college. Voicemail again. Dammit. I dial again. He keeps his phone on vibrate but he usually has it plugged in right next to his pillow, as close to his head as possible. He should be waking up by now. I hang up and dial again. Then, I cut the call short. I should just call the police, shouldn't I? This is insane. Rick's not answering and Happy needs help and somehow I'm the gatekeeper. Happy's stuck in that awful club. She could get hurt. The police should be there. They should help her. But, Happy said the wrong people could get in trouble. If I'm the reason Happy's friends get arrested or deported she'll never speak to me again.

But Happy could get hurt.

I punch in 9 then 1 but stop. I think about before, in the convenience store. The sirens in the background. They were too late then. And what would I tell them anyway? I only know a small fraction of the story. All I can say is there's a woman locked in the basement of some seedy nightclub. It sounds like a bad movie trailer. Why would they believe me? They could pull up my name and immediately know about what happened before. They'd think I was having some kind of psychotic episode. They might just come here instead. I think about calling the anonymous tip line again. But they couldn't help either. Wouldn't. Not unless I was willing to come down to the station or let them poke around here. Maybe they'd send a lone patrolman to check on things. Someone could shoo him away. Happy told me Lee was a smooth-talker. Besides, Happy should call. She wants to. Maybe I shouldn't take that away from her.

I stand up and dial Rick's number again. This time I leave him a voicemail. I tell him the whole story, at least everything Happy told me. I give him the exact details of the telephone conversation with acute accuracy, should anything she said be a clue I may have missed. I tell him to go straight to The Dollhouse, to call me as soon as he leaves. Then, I tell him he's a real fucking prick for not answering his phone the fifth time I try to call him. Then, I hang up and dial again.

I leave another two voicemails. I tell him he's the most unreliable person I've ever met. I tell him he always lets me down. I tell him I'm never working with him again. Then, the balloon in my chest inflates to the point where I can't see straight. Nothing helps. I try to take in a deep breath but I can't. I can't panic, not now. I sit down on the bed, put my head between my legs, letting my arms hang down and touch the floor. I keep the phone in my hand, anticipating the buzz when Rick calls back. But it's cold and still in my sweaty palm.

Why is this happening to me? It's not. It's happening to her.

This is about Happy. She needs help. She needs Rick. Or she needs Rick because she needs me, and because I can't help her, she has to ask for Rick. But she called me because I'm the person she thought to call. This is significant.

I've reached a crossroads. If I take the right-hand path in my mind, I'll step back from all of this, disengage from the insanity, and stay right here. I'll make sure all the windows and doors are locked from the inside and I'll call the police and report it all. My conscience will be clear, I'll be in the safety of my home, and this blemish will fade until it will be as though I were never here in the first place.

The path on the left-hand side is menacing. Maybe I could do this. The words materialize and they feel so alien it's almost like someone else's voice I hear. I look around. It's just me here in the bedroom. My thoughts, my words. What am I thinking? I'm afraid of dying. I do everything I can to avoid injury or illness, putting myself into a situation where I might not be able to get out. But what do I have to show for it? Besides, I want Happy to be safe. Or I want to know Happy is safe or not safe, instead of waiting to hear about it the next day. Maybe I want Happy to be safe and with me. I close my eyes, try to imagine that I'm someone else. Maybe some other version of me — a version of me who can, who does. This time is different.

There's a low roar, something deep within me, tightening down on the inflated ball at the center of my chest. My body fights itself — the bubble might even pop. I can almost breathe again. I get to my feet. My mind spins. The world vibrates. The apartment is smaller than it's ever been.

I call Happy back. Her phone goes straight to voicemail. Her battery must be dead. Her voice recording beeps and I leave her a message: "I'm coming."

Chapter 2

I stand in my living room, arms crossed over my chest, feeling like an alien in a black wool coat I've never worn before. My mother gave it to me for Christmas three years ago, a perfect example of wishful thinking. It's been in the hallway closet ever since. I cut the retail tags off the sleeve before I put it on. I try to swallow. The area I'm headed right now, in the heart of lower downtown, is known for gang activity. There's a report nearly every weekend about some act of violence as people spill out of the bars. Happy couldn't be in a worse location.

I'll have to walk. I could get on one of the mall shuttles at Union Station but it's only a few blocks and the shuttle is free and I don't know what kind of people will be riding so early in the morning. I could call a taxi cab, but that doesn't seem safe either. The thought of getting into a car with a random driver makes my stomach bloat like one of those toys designed to expand when left in a bowl of water. I taste the vinegary burn of unease in the back of my throat. It's not that far anyway, just a little over a mile. I have GPS on my phone. I've never used it before, but I've input the address. It's given me a route. I know where I'm going, or at least the general direction. The lower part of downtown, or "LoDo" as they call it, is fairly compact. I've walked around the area before. But that was forever ago. I shouldn't trust that anything will be the way it was. Besides, it's always good to have a map. There's no telling what will happen once I get down there. I could get lost or turned around. Difficult with the Rocky Mountains always to the west, but still possible.

I check my pockets. I have my key, my cell phone, my wallet. I pull out my black leather billfold. I carry it more out of habit than necessity, since its contents might just as well remain on my dresser as in my back pocket. But I like the feel of it on my person, knowing these items are always with me. My driver's license, which I renewed by mail last year. My credit card. I removed some cash from the emergency stash in the lock box, just in case. I also have a medical information card and an emergency contact card all tucked into the leather slots. At least it will be easy to identify my body.

Should I separate the cash from the credit card? I shouldn't make it easy for a mugger. On the other hand, the convenient location of all my material goods may just be my only salvation from getting shanked. My stomach turns over and I think I might be sick. I put a hand on my abdomen and take a hard swallow. My tongue feels swollen against the roof of my mouth. I move to the kitchen and get myself a glass of water. I'm burning up in this damn coat. The collar scratches the back of my neck. I should have had it dry-cleaned. I just never anticipated it leaving my closet.

What am I doing? I'm wearing a coat, all my things collected, like I'm actually going to step out into the hallway and leave. If I could do this, if I had it in me to just get up and go, I would have done it already. It's not like I've never tried. How many times have I sat with my back pressed to my locked front door, listening for some sign of life on the other side? I accepted the fact a long time ago that sitting with my head pressed up against the door, straining to hear something, was as close as I would ever get.

Now here I am again. I close my eyes. Every muscle in my body tenses with the thought of how many ways this could all go wrong, how many places I could find myself stuck without an exit, the uncountable variables of outside where there's no telling how I will react, and what will come of the situation, of me. I unlock the chains and then the deadbolt and swing the door wide open.

I peer into the hall. It's the same hall I've studied for five and a half years, with its faded carpet and narrow walls. I'm stuck in the doorway, my toes lined up against the edge of the threshold. I might as well be standing at Everest base camp, staring upward.

Look at all the time I've wasted. Something else might have happened to Happy by now. The circumstances, already vague, could have changed. That's all the more reason for me not to go. Out there, anything could go wrong. I could, will, panic. And, then where will I be? How could anyone help me? Moreover, how could I help her? My entire body quakes with the overwhelming urge to step back. But I can't. I have to do this. I glance over my shoulder. The apartment is the same as it's always been. A few slight adjustments over the years, a new couch and coffee table, but for all intents and purposes, it's remained unchanged.

And what about me? I've gotten a few years older, the circles under my eyes are a little darker and my mid-section is just a little softer. But, I've remained here, just as wholly unchanged. It's not the same now. Not since she came here and not since she left. I am not the same. I turn back and face the door.

I imagine that my feet are glued to the floor and it's impossible to propel myself backward. There's a brick wall behind me. Though I can still smell last night's marinara and the air of inside pulls at me, I can believe this. That's right. The only way to go is forward. I lift my leg and take a step, pulling the door closed behind me as I go. One. Then another.

Two.

Three.

I've been counting steps for years, tracking my fitness level on my pedometer. But the pedometer is still on the dresser in the bedroom. I hadn't put it on yet this morning. I can't go back. That's okay. I'll count my own this time. I look down at the floor. Forest green. I'm out in the hall. Three steps over the threshold of my apartment. I run my foot against the worn carpet. Not so different from the rug in my own apartment. That reminds me. I have to lock the door.

I'm afraid that if I turn around I'm going to collapse, but I'm the only one here and it has to be done. I won't be able to lock the chains from the outside. I can't worry about that. I close my eyes and reach into my pocket. I pull out the key. My hand shakes, but I try not to think about it because then I'll look down and seeing the nerves manifest in my quivering arm will tighten the fist in my chest and I have to at least make it down the stairs.

I turn around and face the door, the black mark of spray paint over the peephole. I reach out and try to slide the key into the lock but my hand shakes and I miss the keyhole. I drop the key.

"Shit." I straighten up and look around the hallway because my key is on the floor and the door's not locked. I wish now, more than ever, that someone was here to help me. Fuck Rick. At this point it would be just as easy to reach out, turn the knob, and get myself back inside. No. I take a deep breath, let my shoulders rise and chest puff out, then I exhale and bend over to retrieve my key. I peel it off of the carpet and stand up, perhaps a little too fast, because the white patches flash in front of my eyes. No. I smack my cheek. The key's in my hand and I feel the metal teeth scrape my skin. Ouch. This is good. Something real to focus on. I wonder if I drew blood as I reach out and slide the key into the lock. I turn it and then I check the doorknob, jiggle it with a desperate ferocity. I'm not sure if I'm checking to make sure that it's locked or hoping that it's not. It doesn't budge. That settles that. I put the key back into my pocket and reach up to touch the scratch. Just a thin raised line. I didn't break the skin. I face the hallway. It's time to go. I turn, counting my steps, focused on each action.

I'm on the third floor of a three-story building. There are four apartments on each floor, two on each side of the hall. My apartment is in the back left corner. The stairwell is at the front right of the hall. 11 steps to the first flight of stairs. I grip the railing. I shouldn't have done that. Who knows how many people have touched it. I bet the cleaning crew doesn't even mess with the stairs. There's a few pieces of trash, a crinkled fast food wrapper in the corner. But the railing is firm and sturdy under my hand. I need the support. I take one slow step at a time. It's a relatively steep staircase. I could break something. Wouldn't that be perfect after I've already come all this way? I take small strides across the landing that separates the flights of stairs. By the time I hit ground level, I'm at 41 steps. At least I'm getting in some exercise. When I let go of the railing, I can feel the slimy film of filth, mixed with my own sweat, on the sticky skin of my palm. I wipe it against my coat. Now it will definitely need to be dry-cleaned.

I step into the lobby and pause on step 48, hover at the doorway — a heavy, metal door that leads out onto a wide, concrete sidewalk. It bothered me that the apartment didn't have any kind of locked entry, but rent is expensive in the city, and the price was right. At the time, I was still making those kinds of compromises. I haven't seen this entryway in five years. The mailboxes are on the wall across from me, large boxes with silver doors. Happy had been collecting the mail for me. I need to get moving. I push through one of the wooden doors and step out onto the concrete. The cold bites my cheeks, the tips of my fingers. I forgot to dig around for my old pair of gloves.

I pause just outside the doorway and take a few deep breaths. The cold stings the inside of my nose so I try breathing through my mouth. My breath comes out in wet puffs. From this side of the building, I'm surrounded by other buildings. To the right of the inconspicuous door that leads to the apartments is a storefront that takes up the ground floor of my building. When I moved in, it had been the office for a non-profit arts organization. Now it's the home of some kind of trendy clothing boutique. It's not open, nor are most of the other stores on the street. It's too early.

The only place with any sign of life is the coffee shop across the street to the left. It doesn't look open yet, but a few lights are on inside. Someone must be getting ready. It's been here for years, a local favorite. When I first moved in, I visited once. They made a decent soy cambric and I liked how they displayed the work of local artists on a rotating schedule. But it was crowded and noisy and full of teens. I never went back.

A man walks past me, bundled in his own heavy coat. He holds it closed against his neck with hands in thick gloves. He wears a red and black flannel hat with earflaps. He comes prepared for this early December morning. I watch his feet move up and down as he hurries by, the white rim of his Converse sneakers peeking out from the hem of his jeans every time he lifts his legs. His steps are confident, assured. I can walk like that, feel like that. Or at least I can pretend. For Happy. I force myself to take step 67 in the opposite direction.

To the left of my apartment building is a monstrous apartment complex complete with a private parking garage and all the best in luxury amenities. The complex is separated into two equally large buildings by a concrete path that connects the bridge over the highway to the bridge over the river. I need to cross the latter in order to cut through the park. I turn down the concrete and head east. About halfway down the walkway, I look up from the ground in front of me. The apartments each have balconies, wrapped in tinsel garlands and strands of Christmas lights. Some of the lights have been turned off. Some are still lit. White, blue, multi-colored strands in varying shapes and sizes. There's no rhyme or reason to the color, the scheme. I think of the Kandinksy, of being back in the warmth of my apartment.

I stop. Double over. I might be sick. It's like someone has taken my stomach and tried to roll it up like an old newspaper. I put my hands on my knees, wait for the sickness to rise in my throat. Nothing happens. I take a few more breaths through my mouth. I can't do this. My body fights against every step I take in the opposite direction of home. It's telling me that I'm not ready. Happy's biggest mistake wasn't going back to the club, it was thinking I could be more than just a body crumpling in on itself like an imploding building. I'm going to disappoint her again.

Down the street toward the park, I can see the outline of a couple nestled in the dark shadows of the bridge over the river, holding one another. It's hard to discern anything about them in the still-dark morning, to see where one stops and the other begins. They are a single entity pressed up against the railing. The soles of my feet begin to itch. I'm a trespasser, spying on an intimate moment I have no right to witness. I'm baking in this coat, unable to look away. I feel the heat creeping up my neck and cheeks. The contrast makes the air on my exposed skin feel even colder. I should turn back, retrace the 193 steps that have gotten me this far out into the chaos.

The couple breaks apart. They're a young couple, early twenties. The man takes the woman's hand and pulls her away from the railing. She pushes off with a start and her playful laughter echoes. She's almost tripping over her feet as she follows him. They take off down the path that cuts through the park and I watch them until they are obscured by the trees. They're exploring the city, as well as each other. Happy and I were doing something like that for a little while. That newness was almost enough. But novelty always wears away with time, and time goes by too fast in a one bedroom apartment. I stopped trying to be new the second she handed me the spare key. But I never thought she'd cease being new as well. That she'd go back to the place she was before. Am I at fault for that?

I pull out my cellphone. It's a little past 7:00 am. I've wasted an hour of her time already. No missed calls. Not from Happy and not from Rick. Happy said her battery was dying. I decide to give Rick another try. Could he have gone straight there after receiving my voicemails and just not bothered to call me back? That's not unlike him. But Happy would have called. She'd probably assume I'd called the cops by now. But I'm not going to. Not yet.

Rick's phone goes to voicemail. I leave one last message. "I'm walking to get Happy now."

That's right. I'm walking. At least that's what I'm trying to do. I think about the look on Rick's face when he hears this message. I hope he drops his iPhone. He hates the way those plastic protective cases look. The impact might crack the screen. That would serve him right for not answering in the first place. I make for the bridge a little quicker.

The bridge is wide, so I can walk straight down the center and I won't be close to the edge on either side. It boasts a sturdy looking metal framework, including two tall, arching beams that stand at the halfway point across the Platte. Still, this metal framework is overlaid with slats of wood—not real wood, a synthetic plastic that's meant to look similar to wood. I suppose it's meant to add to the scenic charm of this urban park. The slats are positioned tightly together and the metal framework runs underneath the whole structure. And yet, I can't shake the feeling that something could go wrong and I could end up in the icy water below. Maybe it's the fact that, on top of the slats, this is a cable-stayed bridge. Three cables extend from both sides of each hulking white beam and connect to the bridge below. What if one of these cables were to snap? I take a step back. That's ridiculous. The stay cables are designed to hold immense amounts of weight, far more than this pedestrian bridge ever sees in foot and bicycle traffic combined. It's far more likely one of the slats will fall out.

That's not helpful. Nor is it true. Besides, if I'm going to get to Happy, I have to cross the bridge regardless. I reach out my foot and tap the first slat. It doesn't waver. It's strong. Even if one of the slats did somehow break and manage to fall into the river—which seems relatively impossible—the individual slats are so narrow that I couldn't even fit my foot through sideways. That's right. There's no reason this bridge is any less safe than any other bridge, and people walk across bridges in cities all around the world every day and they are mostly fine. I take a few steps. It's a little disorienting, the way it feels underfoot, but I adjust my gait so that the ball of my foot comes down firmly on the center of a slat with every step. I barely feel the tiny space between each one. I make it halfway across the bridge when I misstep and the ball of my foot comes straight down on a crack.

I look down. The slats are so close together you can hardly see the space between them. Yet I catch a little glimpse of the slow moving water below. I start to feel like I'm standing on the deck of a ship, and my body has to move with the rocking motion or I might fall over. I'm not swaying, not really, because this bridge is strong and unwavering, but my knees might buckle. I try to shake the feeling off. My vision distorts and the slats beneath my feet look closer than they did a second ago. I'm either falling or they're rising up to meet me. I close my eyes and stand still for a long time. I listen to the sound of the river. I think of Happy, try to imagine what she might do if she were standing beside me. She'd probably start tapping her foot. She'd be right. I need to hurry. When I open my eyes I haven't moved and neither has the bridge. I take off again, keeping my eyes fixed on the park just beyond, where the yellowed grass sticks out through the thin layer of snow. I hold my breath and don't look down again.

At 503 steps I'm on the other side. Spots like shooting stars flash across my line of sight. They remind me to breathe and I let out a whistle of air as my cheeks deflate. There's a few benches on either side of me, bolted down to the Redstone platform that lines either side of this end of the bridge. I think about sitting. I could use a chance to catch my breath. But the way my body sags, as though gravity has shifted and presses down harder than it ever has before, suggests that if I sit down, I might not get back up. She doesn't have time for that.

The concrete path through the park isn't quite a straight shot, but there are no blind corners either. I curve around the trees and walk along the sidewalk. The sun is just starting to come up but the streetlamps are still on. You can almost see the particles of artificial light fight against the natural glow that's overtaking the morning.

Chapter 3

It's hard to believe that in a city close to the center of a landlocked state, there's another fucking bridge. This bridge, the Millennium Bridge, is even bigger than the first one. In fact, the mast is over two hundred feet tall. How could I have forgotten this? It looms, drawing attention away from the skyline, every time I look out my window. Every aspect of the design is both stunning and horrifying. It towers so far above the ground that it takes three flights of concrete steps, each separated by a wide landing, to even reach the bridge itself. The good news is it's suspended by triple the number of cables as the bridge I managed to cross.

It's now 7:27 am. This means it's taken me almost half an hour to walk about half a mile. This also means just about anything could have happened to Happy by now. I grasp the metal railing that runs down the center of the wide flights. Each step gets a little harder as I continue upward, until I'm grasping the railing with both hands like I'm pulling myself up by rope. By the time I reach the top of the staircase at 975 steps, I'm drenched in sweat and the heat of my coat mixed with the biting morning air makes me simultaneously hot and cold. I better be careful.

When glass is subjected to this kind of extreme temperature, it tends to shatter. I wipe the sweat off my forehead and take a few sharp breaths, try to regroup. I'm at the start of the bridge, planted at the very center.

I look out across the bridge at the skyline. The sky has a dusty orange aura that frames the buildings in the hazy dawn light. The sun's meant to fool. It's cold outside. I've felt this cold creeping into cracks under the windows and door for weeks. Now being out in it feels like I've never felt real cold before. A far cry from my climate-controlled apartment. I clench my hands into tight fists, feel my nails digging into the palms of my hands, try to squeeze the cold out of my fingertips. It doesn't help. I could get frostbite out here on a morning like this. I should get inside before it's too late. Then again, the windows in my living room face west and I haven't seen the sunrise in a long time.

Anyway, the sooner I cross, the sooner I can get to the Dollhouse. What then? Will she be all right? I can't think about that right now. All I can do is keep walking. I take off across the bridge. As I focus on my feet—up, down, up, down—I feel the roar that presses from inside. I can do this. I stick to the center of the bridge and walk as straight a line as possible until I hit the staircase on the other side. I take a tentative step down, my hand sliding along the cold metal railing as I go. When I get down to street level, I stop and rub my hands together, try to warm them up.

There's the bus depot and the train tracks, a parking lot to my left. Beyond that, Union Station, Denver's first train depot, stands erect, a giant orange sign attached to the façade. It's a striking old building, crafted out of a strange kind of limestone—Yule Marble—that can only be found in a specific location in the West Elk Mountains. In Colorado, everything ties back to the mountains. I wish I could be as certain about what was happening to Happy as I am about that.

I move to the street corner and press the "walk" light. The heart of the city still feels some distance away. I have to walk two blocks down 16th street until I hit the red brick buildings close to where I'm going. The light changes and the white "walk" sign illuminates on the other side of the street. My feet are cemented to the curb. There's a car pulling up to the red light. What if the person's in a hurry or on his cell phone? What if he doesn't see me? I look across the street. It seems so far. Four blocks up 16th street and then three blocks to the left down Blake before I'm even at The Dollhouse. And then what? How will I help her?

The pedestrian sign has changed back into a red hand telling me to stop. I never started. I'll have to wait through the next cycle of lights. I take a deep breath. Denver is not like New York or other larger metropolitan areas. It knows its place as a western city. It's more spread out, more evenly distributed somehow. It pales in comparison to walking around Manhattan. My father took me once, when I was in high school. He was there on business and it was one of those rare attempts he made to connect. He'd spent so much of my childhood not understanding me, trying to calm my mother's every little worry in regards to me, that by my teenage years, I think he'd grown tired of me. At the very least, he didn't know what to do with me.

He'd made plans for us to eat nice dinners and see a couple of shows after he finished his meetings. He expected me to entertain myself during the day. He left me with plenty of cash, told me to take a cab somewhere, see whatever I wanted. I'd been excited. So many museums. But I was also anxious—always anxious. We stayed in a swanky hotel on the same block as Grand Central Station. That first morning, I walked outside with a city map in hand. I'd planned on visiting the Met first. I'd grab breakfast on the way. Then, I'd tackle MoMa the next day. Hoards of morning commuters were coming from the trains. They bubbled up onto the streets in droves. I'd never seen anything like it. I pressed my back against the marble exterior of the towering hotel and froze. I looked through the moving masses to the street where cars were deadlocked, horns honking, with yellow cabs sticking out at awkward angles into the wrong lanes of traffic. I went back upstairs and ordered room service. I didn't leave the hotel without my father the rest of the trip.

The light flashes to "walk" again. Denver is nothing like that. I can count a total of five people within eyesight. Morning traffic hasn't even really hit yet. I can do this. I swallow hard, think about what it looks like when an hourglass is turned over and the sand begins to funnel in a thin stream to the other side. My legs are light enough to move. I step off the curb and hurry across the street. I set my sights on the brick buildings ahead of me and make it to the next street. I cross without stopping. Thank God. If I stop now, I'm not sure I can start again.

At 1,551 steps, I hit Blake Street. I want to call Happy, send her a text, tell her that I'm on the way, that I'm almost there. But her phone might already be dead. A few more people mill about this part of town. A man with a briefcase passes me to the right. A woman moves by on the left. Her hair is pulled back and she's wearing tight leggings and tennis shoes. A yoga mat sticks out of the corner of her giant tote bag. A young man with a beard and a crudely hand-knitted ski cap rides past on his bicycle—brave considering there are still patches of ice on the sidewalk. There's something comforting in the perfunctory feel of this movement.

I make it two whole blocks. Not far now. I push forward, push through the pressure that's welling up in every part of me, making my limbs feel swollen and stiff. I'm roasting. My body is a hot air balloon. I take heavier steps, press myself into the ground, almost stomp my feet, afraid I might float away. At 2,051 steps, I'm standing in front of the Dollhouse.

Chapter 4

The Dollhouse hides in a nondescript building of red brick. The façade belongs to a sports bar, The Batting Cage—a fitting name for an establishment only a couple blocks from the baseball stadium. It isn't what I expected. We're not in some red light district. No XXX signs as I look down the block. No additional gentleman's clubs. Instead, restaurants, bars, and a few shops line the ground level, with offices and lofts above and below. Just like every other block in LoDo. The stadium—a brick edifice with purple and forest green paint—looms several blocks away. The main entrance to the club is just a door with the building number posted above. No flashy sign or any kind of identifying features. I wonder how many people even know it's here.

Only upon closer inspection am I able to find the back entrance. I trail the side of the building, staying close to the brick. At the end of the alley, I come to a small parking lot. Just one car, a lime green Beetle. Probably not Lee's. About a third of the way down the wall is a metal door. There's a trash dumpster, a stack of cardboard boxes flattened and stuffed behind it. The area reeks of old garbage. Broken bottles line the asphalt. It's a disgusting mess. Could this be an indication of what I'm going to find inside? It doesn't matter. Happy's inside.

I pull on the door, just in case. Of course it's locked. My stomach begins to churn, like storm clouds moving across a darkening sky. But how can I find her without a clue as to what might be waiting? It's like that final step off the side of a cliff, the rushing water below. I take a deep breath, try to imagine another version of myself, one that doesn't feel like he's up to his knees in sinking sand.

I'm afraid to knock — people shouldn't know I'm here. I could look for a different entrance, but this seems irresponsible — even dangerous. I stuff my hands into the pockets of my wool coat and try to imagine what Rick would do, what anyone else might do in this situation. I'm too far out of my element. I shouldn't be here. I can't even bring myself to knock on a locked door. Happy needs someone better than that.

But it is just me here. I came all this way — 2,145 steps — and the absurdity of turning back at this point is enough to tighten my hand into a fist. I start pounding on the door. There's nothing else I can do. I pound hard, harder than I should, because focusing on that feeling means I'm not thinking about what's going to happen if the door does open. I've been pounding for a solid minute when the door flies open with such force that I have to take a step backward. A petite blonde with black streaks in her straight hair and a diamond stud in her nose stands in the doorway. She's wearing short black shorts with fishnet stockings underneath. Even with her gray, high-heeled boots, she's almost a foot shorter than me. Her top is a tight fitting burgundy sweater vest pulled over a white dress shirt.

"Can I help you?" Her voice reminds me of a baby raccoon my father found trapped under the shifting foundation of our family home, when I was six or seven. My mother was afraid to let me play in the backyard for a month—rabies.

"Can you let me in?" I manage between swallows. My tongue is chalky, like I've just inhaled a mouthful of dust.

She pauses and shifts her weight so one hip juts out in a sharp curve. She lets her hand rest there. "What?"

"It's cold."

She gives me a long, sideways glance, narrowing her eyes as she looks me up and down. Then, she smiles. "You're a little early for the tour. I barely got my coat off." She looks at the silver watch she wears on her left wrist. "I thought you said 8:30."

"What?" It's my turn to be confused.

"I'm Jean." She extends her hand. Her nails are painted charcoal gray. "We spoke on the phone, Mr. Lang."

I almost tell her that I have no idea what she's talking about, that we've never spoken and I'm not the person she thinks I am, when I realize what's happening. She's confused me for someone else. Someone who's supposed to be here. This is exactly the excuse I need to get inside and find Happy. I stick out my hand and give a quick squeeze, releasing before she has a chance to notice the nervous perspiration.

"Come in," she says, stepping aside. The doorway now stands open in front of me. I force my foot across the threshold and step inside. She closes the door behind me. "We're so pleased you're considering The Dollhouse for your event. I can promise you a top notch experience unlike any other."

She starts down a narrow corridor with black-and-white checkered flooring and red and black walls. Two doors on either side are marked with gold stars. The hallway seems deceptively clean but I know that every surface is covered in the grime of what goes on here. My skin tingles as though I can actually feel the bacteria as it streams across the surface of my skin. I take a deep breath and grit my teeth, try to shake it off.

"Dressing rooms," she says, "for the female staff."

I nod. Where Happy used to get ready. Where is she now? We creep past a closed door with a frosted glass window and large gold letters that read *Raymond Abano.* I remember that name. He's the owner. Two more offices, both with closed doors. I wonder if one of these belongs to Lee. He could be in there right now. The wool collar of my coat itches the back of my neck. I look at my feet, focus on the steps, visualize the count like an Excel spreadsheet in my head. There was only one car in the parking lot.

Jean turns and smiles at me. "This way," she says, with a slight jerk of her head.

We walk to the end of the hall and I look around for a staircase. Happy said she was on a lower level somewhere. We step out into a round, open room, something straight out of the Moulin Rouge, with mirrored walls, plushy sofas, and burgundy and gold tapestries. An antique chandelier dangles from the ceiling. To the left is an opening exposing dark wooden tables and stools, with floor to ceiling shelves of liquor nestled against the back wall. Poles for dancers are mounted on risers throughout the space. Hallways fork in three directions, including the one we just came from. She could be down any of those halls. If she's even still here. Who knows what could have happened by now? I can't think like that. She has to be here. I resist the urge to call out her name. I need to be careful.

"That's the bar." Jean points where I've been looking, and I remember that I'm supposed to be on a tour. I give an exaggerated nod, as though I've just fallen asleep standing up. Jean closes one eye and gives me a pinched expression. Too dramatic. Now she's onto me. I'm going to get kicked out before I even get a chance to find the stairs. My stomach twists at the thought of coming so far, being so close to Happy, and still not finding her. I raise a closed fist to my mouth and clear my throat. This seems to refocus her energy on the tour. She points to the first hallway to the right of the open bar space. "Down there we have private rooms for one-on-one striptease, fetish play, two-way mirrors. That sort of thing."

I try another nod, much smaller this time. I do a quick scan for any suspicious looking doors or secret passageways. I don't see anything that stands out as more dubious than the rest of this place. I wish Happy would have told me where I was supposed to go. But she was trying to hurry. I wish I would have thought to ask her.

"The second hall has the cross-dressing salon and guest lockers."

"Organized," I say. I'd imagined a sort of raunchy free-for-all.

She flashes me another smile. "If you rent out the entire space, you'll have full access to any of these areas. We'll be fully staffed with our best girls and I can assure you this will be a truly unforgettable bachelor party. Your friend will be in very good hands." As she says this last part, she takes a step backward to stand beside me. She wraps her arm through mine.

I jump backward with such force I almost knock her over. Her face is like a small animal who's just been caught in the beam of a flashlight. Under different circumstances, I might laugh at the thought that anybody could be frightened by me. But not now. "I'm sorry," I say.

"That's all right," she says in her squirrely voice. She clears her throat. "Should we go to my office? I have some forms for you to look over."

I walked into this lie. What do I do now? "Where's the brothel?" I ask her. Her expression flickers in surprise. Maybe nobody says 'brothel' anymore.

"Excuse me?" she asks. Then, she shakes her head. "You never mentioned you were one of our VIP customers." Her eyes narrow and surprise and suspicion merge in the creases of her forehead.

"Well, I am."

She raises her eyebrows. "But you haven't taken advantage of our services?"

I thrust my hands in the pocket of my coat and shrug my shoulders. "I'm new to this," I say. Not a lie.

She pauses a moment, gives me a hard stare. My stomach tightens. I've never been very good at lying. Then, just when I think she might call my bluff and kick me out, she shrugs her shoulders and continues. "We have a secure entry located at the end of that hallway there. There would be an additional fee."

I don't understand any of this. I look around. I have to get out of here as fast as I can. But I have to find Happy first. I can't keep this up any longer. "I'm not Mr. Lang," I say.

She blinks, gives a small nod, like she's confirming some secret detail in her head. "Didn't think so."

"I know Happy."

"Happy Lafferty?" She squints in confusion but her eyelids flutter open. "What the fuck is going on?"

Where to start? "She's here. Locked in. I have to get her." I try to take a gasp of air between each sentence, because I'm finding it harder to catch my breath, my chest constricting with every word. I can't panic. Not now.

"I don't—"

"Where's the key?" I ask her.

"It's in Ray's office, but…"

"Can you get it?"

"I—"

"Please?" The desperation fractures my voice. The way she looks at me, her eyes welling with conflict, she hears it too.

"Okay," she says. "This way."

We head back to the staff hallway and come to stand before the door with gold lettering. "I'll go find the keys. Stay on the lookout."

If I see anybody, we're in trouble whether I'm standing here or not. I put my back to the wall, feeling more secure with a solid surface behind me. I scan the hall in either direction and realize how exposed I am. Anyone could come from the staff entrance on one end, or the main parlor on the other. I close my eyes. I almost hear the creaking door from the parking lot, Lee's voice from the entry. I'll be found and destroyed out here in the hallway. I'm not going to make it out of this alive. Pain surges against my rib cage like a constricting blood pressure cuff that doesn't release.

After a minute, Jean opens the door and the sound of the turning knob tears through my stomach, like someone jumping rope with my intestines. "Found them." She jangles the keychain on her index finger and extends her hand for me to take them.

"You should go." I don't know why I say this. Clearly she knows what goes on here. I shouldn't do her any favors. Still, she was professional and courteous and she helped me when she could have refused. Maybe the reason she came to be here is as complicated as it was for Happy. Maybe she's one of the girls Happy tried to warn. "We're going to call the police."

She gives a sullen nod and turns to return to her office. She pauses at the door. "I hope she's okay," she says. Then, she disappears and closes the door behind her.

I head back to the parlor, zigzagging across the maze of erotic excess, until I enter the hallway where Jean had pointed. I come to an inconspicuous wooden door at the end of the hall, spaced farther from the others along the hallway. It's marked *Private*. Nothing out of the ordinary. No peephole or prison bars. There are several keys on the key-ring. I fumble through them, trying each with trembling fingers. The fifth one slides into the lock and turns. I open the door and realize I've found what I'm looking for. Under the flickering glow of an overhead light is a concrete staircase. My hands sting, like they're latex gloves inflated with hot air. I ball them into fists at my sides.

"Who's there?" A voice calls up from below. Happy.

I hurry down the stairs. I take the last step down onto the concrete floor. The dull lighting casts a somber pallor over the entire space—her skin, her hands, have a grayish glow under the beams—a stark contrast from the romantic mood lighting of the fantasy world upstairs. But the men who come here aren't paying for the allure. This large room has a few cushioned chairs against one wall. A waiting room? There are three doors along the far wall. Those must be the rooms with the beds. The smell of baby powder and body spray mixes with the underlying odor of sweat and sex. The thought of being trapped in this room with no windows makes my stomach lurch. Happy's sitting against the wall in the corner. She wears blue jeans and a purple sweater. Even in the dull lighting, I can see her hair's tangled in her face, her mascara smeared under her eyes.

When she spots me, her face tightens like she's staring at an apparition that's just passed through the wall. "Fuck me," she says.

"Hi." It's the best I can do. My chest tightens and my head throbs and I'm going to lose the battle to my body. I can't hold the panic back any longer.

"When I called, I didn't think…" She trails off. She doesn't move. I can't move. So we stay suspended with all the distance of this dirty room between us. "I wasn't trying to make you feel like you had to…" She pauses. Then she's on her feet and crossing the room and wrapping her arms around me. I don't tell her that it's killing me to stand here, looking at all this filth, with us holding each other in the middle. I don't say anything. She pulls out of my arms. Her forehead wrinkles as she blinks. "Thank you," she whispers.

"Okay."

She smiles and her eyes are a mixture of sadness and gratitude, like the brownish result of two poorly blended dabs of paint. I just want to touch her again, to kiss her, to hold her, but I don't. She doesn't give me the chance. Something shifts and her expression hardens into something like determination. "Let's get the hell out of here," she says, reaching for my hand.

"I can't," I say, and that's it. The panic crashes in on me like a tidal wave. It's enough to push me backward, until I'm pressed against the wall. I slide down onto the concrete floor and put my head between my knees. I might pass out from the pain in my chest, my cramping stomach, everywhere. I've lost complete control. Blackness curls inward from the corners of my eyes like charred paper. Lee will find me passed out on the floor when he comes back. What will he do to me then?

"Not now, Wes," she says, coming over to where I sit on the ground.

"I can't get up." I can't even breathe. "Just go without me."

I manage to look up at her. Her narrow frame trembles in the shadow cast from the harsh light. She's terrified. Still, she comes and sits down beside me anyway. She'll ignore her own fear and help me with my own.

"It's going to be okay," she says. She places her hand in mine. "You can do this."

If only I were as permeable as my cells. Imagine if Happy's

courage could pass through her warm hand and into my own. I blink away the blinding flashes that fight to blur my vision, making it harder and harder to keep my eyes open.

She squeezes my hand tighter. "Did I mention how glad I am that you're here?"

While the statistical probability is astronomical that it's sheer adrenaline talking, it's good to hear her say it. Besides, the heat of her hand in mine—the energy that passes between us—is enough to get me back on my feet.

"Okay," I say. I push myself up against the wall and stand to go, but I hear footsteps on the stairs. Oh god.

"What the hell?" The man standing at the bottom of the steps is not Lee. He wears a tailored gray suit with a bright green tie. His dark, curled hair is combed back with gel. "Jesus, Happy, it's good to see you on your feet. Lee made it sound like he killed you."

"Thanks for your concern, Ray." Happy feigns nonchalance, but her voice splits. "We were just leaving." Happy tries to sidestep her old boss, but he cuts her off.

"Who's your friend?" he asks, and then before she can answer he steps over to me and puts out his hand. "I'm Raymond Abano. This is my club."

This is not the time for introductions. I don't say anything and I ignore his hand.

He turns to Happy. "Your protection?" He gives her a smile. He seems at ease despite the subsurface particles of anxiety that fill the room with an electric intensity.

"Cut the bullshit, Ray." Happy's voice has gone up in pitch.

"Like I said, we're leaving."

"Wait." He takes a step forward. It's a slight movement, but it shifts his whole demeanor. Gone is the calm, the smile. "Let's talk about this. Maybe in my office? Your friend is welcome to join us."'

"Too late." Happy crosses her arms. "I'll call 911 right now." She pulls out her cell phone. But her battery is dead. I have my phone too, in my pocket, but every joint in my body feels locked and I don't think I could force myself to reach for it.

"Don't." He puts his arms up. "What we're doing here, it's not what you think. Nobody's been coerced. The girls participate of their own free will. There's no need to overreact."

Happy shakes her head. "You can't honestly believe that."

"You don't know what you're talking about." He gives a shrug of his shoulders but there's a sharpness in the action that is the opposite of composed.

Happy's voice drops lower. "You have daughters, Ray."

Ray's eyes widen and he holds Happy's gaze for just a moment. There's something like sadness in the slow breath he takes. But he clenches his fists at his sides. "You worked here."

Happy's shoulders slump and all the life goes out of her, like a marionette doll with cut strings. We stand in a few moments of silence, waiting to see who'll speak next, when a voice calls down from the top of the stairs. "Fuck, Ray, is she breathing?"

Lee. When he appears at the foot of the staircase, it's clear he's drunk. He sways on his feet, steadies himself. Then, he sees Happy. His eyes pop open like a spring-loaded toy. He steps toward her. "You're okay."

"Don't touch me." Happy takes a step back so she's standing next to me.

"Oh fuck, I'm sorry." He keeps coming. "I'm so sorry. I—"

"You should be." The anger explodes from my mouth.

His eyes settle on me. "What did you say?" He takes a step forward. He looks around the room, from Ray to Happy, then back to me. The lines of his face harden and he bristles. He takes a step closer. The smell of whiskey wafts off his clothes, his breath. "You're a creepy fuck."

I'm about to be murdered. He's going to tear me apart with his bare hands. I imagine him coming at me like a grizzly bear, his weight slamming into me, knocking me to the cement floor. The pain in my abdomen is so great I have to suck in my stomach, tighten the muscles, just to keep myself upright.

"Stop it, Lee." Ray puts his hand on his shoulder and yanks backward. Lee stumbles a little but regains his footing. "It's over."

"But—" Lee tries to pull away but Ray keeps hold. I notice the gold wedding band on his outstretched hand. This is a family man. Nothing makes sense in this place.

Ray looks at Happy. "Go." There's a breathy quality in his voice that can only be describe as tired. "Just get out of here."

He doesn't have to tell me again. I take Happy's hand and pull her toward the stairs. By the time we reach the top, my legs are a tuning fork and I'm barely able to keep myself upright. It feels like dirty sheets are spinning in a washer inside my chest. Happy squeezes my hand as we move through the empty club and out the front door. We make it to the sidewalk and I let go.

"Holy fucking Christ." I know that voice. I blink through my blurring vision to see Rick getting out of his silver 1994 Volvo 850 with blue leather interior, the same car he's been driving since college. He comes over to where we stand on the sidewalk and looks at me like he's seeing me for the first time. "Are you for real?"

I look at him and Happy and then back at the door where I've just come from. "I forgot what step I'm on," I say, and then I lurch forward and vomit all over the concrete.

Chapter 5

"Are you okay?" Happy's on her knees, crouching beside me, her hand on my back. She rubs a pattern of small circles between my shoulder blades. Rick's standing over us with his hands pressed together. They rest against his lips likes he's saying some kind of silent prayer.

"No." I try to blink, avoid looking at the mess. I bend over and heave again, managing to vomit in almost the same location as the first time. After a few moments, I step back and sit down against the side of the building. If I don't move, I should be fine.

"I can't believe it," Rick says, rocking back on his feet. "When I got your voicemail, I didn't think there was any way." He's pacing along the curb where the Volvo still idles. "I almost stopped at your apartment first but I came straight here like you said. What the fuck is going on?"

He looks at Happy this time.

"Why didn't you answer your phone?" I don't look at him. Instead, I focus on the cloud of exhaust trailing from the back of the Volvo. Droplets of condensation drip off the opening of the pipe. There's something soothing about watching them drip, one after another, to the asphalt.

"I'm sorry," he says. "I turned it off after I left your apartment." He shrugs his shoulders. "I'm here now."

"Okay," I say. He's right. He came. "Thank you."

"We should go." Happy steps between the two of us. "Can you give us a lift?"

"Sure thing." Rick's already moving around toward the driver's side door. "Where are we going?"

Happy doesn't pause. "My dad's store."

"We need to call the police," I say. Has everyone forgotten about that?

"I will." Happy bends down and looks at me. "In the car, okay?"

I look over at the Swedish wonder. The vehicle was made for Rick. He's been driving it for a decade and minus a few hiccups, a replaced timing belt, it's been as faithful as his Absolut vodka. It's not like I haven't ridden in it before. Rick was always willing to take me to the grocery store if I needed laundry soap or the student health center if I thought my cold was viral meningitis. I hated the car then; it seems impossible to get inside it now. Still, Volvo people are Volvo people for life, right? It's been reliable.

I put my hand over my mouth because I don't want Happy to smell my breath. "Do I have to?"

"Just get in." Rick's always been sensitive about his car. Or maybe he's nervous about where we're sitting right now. He's right to be.

I get to my feet and move for the passenger side door. I slide onto the seat and close my eyes, ignoring the chill of the creaky leather against my thighs, the creeping feeling that the car is sucking me in. Happy climbs in the backseat.

Rick sits upright, buoyant in the driver's seat. The car lurches forward as he shifts. I retch. It's been so long since I've heard the roar of an engine up close like this. It's different from the distant grumble of souped-up low riders, or the occasional motorcycle I sometimes hear through closed windows. It's too close for comfort. I try to swallow this thought. If I vomit in Rick's car, he's going to get cranky.

With trembling fingers, I manage to fasten my seatbelt, tug on the strap a few times. The security of a buckle that's over ten years old is questionable. Not to mention the fact that there have been leaps and bounds made in the realm of automotive safety over the last decade. As he pulls away from the curb, I grip the door handle and press back in my seat, closing my eyes. Not that this will do me any good. The car's so old, the airbags might not even deploy. In a head-on collision, my neck will snap on the dashboard.

Happy leans forward. "Can I borrow your phone?"

I'm not sure who she's asking, but Rick reaches for his, which sits in the cupholder, and hands it back to her without a word.

"Thanks," she says, and leans back against her seat. She dials and when someone picks up on the other end she says "I need to report a crime." I hope they're more helpful than they have been with me.

I reach into the glove box where I know Rick always keeps a pack of gum. I have to get the taste of vomit out of my mouth or I'm liable to get sick all over again. I take a piece from a package of sugar-free wintergreen. I unwrap the rectangular piece and pop it in my mouth, move it around on either side, chew so hard my teeth clank together. That's a little better. Happy's describing the events that have just transpired in the background. I close my eyes and try to imagine that I'm sitting on the sofa in my living room.

Rick turns right. I feel it, though I refuse to watch. If I'm to become another statistic in automotive deaths, I'd rather not see the oncoming headlights. I feel him staring. I crack an eye and see him facing forward, both hands on the steering wheel, glancing over every few seconds, as if I am an explosive device and he's watching the countdown, unsure of whether or not we'll make it before the big kaboom. He grips the wheel so tight his bones might poke through the skin of his knuckles.

"It's been a long time since you've been in the passenger seat," he says finally.

"Not long enough."

Rick looks at me for too long, smiles.

"What?" I say when I can't stand the stand the staring any longer.

"Nothing," he says. "Just relax."

The electricity that twinges every molecule of the air around us suggests this is something neither of us can do. I press my forehead against the cold glass of the window, take a deep breath.

Happy tells the operator where we're headed, gives them the address. Then, she hangs up. "They're sending officers to the Dollhouse—like anyone will still be there. But it's okay. At least someone knows now." She sits back against the seat and takes a deep breath. "They're also going to send officers to meet us at the store. Take down our statements."

"I want to go home." I want to crawl into my bed and sleep for days.

Happy catches my gaze in the rearview mirror. "You have to make a statement."

"I don't want to." I turn and look at her over my shoulder. "They can come talk to me at the apartment."

Happy lets out a heavy sigh. "You're already here, Wes."

I'm about to say something, when Rick chimes in. "She's got a point."

"Who asked you?" Rick gives me a harsh look and veers slightly to the right.

"Watch it." I grab the dashboard. He's too close to the cars whizzing beside me.

"I've done this before," he says. So my depth perception's a little off.

"We're going to my dad's store, okay?" Happy's voice cracks. I look back at her and see that tears have welled up in her eyes. I didn't mean to make her cry. I've been so focused on my own frame of mind, the fear, that I've forgotten about how she must be feeling right now. Of course she wants to go to her father.

"I'm sorry," I tell her.

"It's okay." She gives me a half-smile and wipes her eyes. Then, she reaches forward and squeezes my shoulder. "Thank you," she says.

The car settles into silence as we drive past the Capitol building headed down Colfax. The sun pours over the side of the giant bronze dome, shading the steps, but I search for the marker—5,280 feet—anyway. I can't see it as we pass, but I know where it is. I picture it in my head. I've never been able to explain why this has mattered to me, living a mile high. I suppose it makes even my life seem bigger somehow.

Lafferty's is in the Washington Park neighborhood. It should take us fifteen minutes to get there. Rick settles into the confident repose of someone who knows where he's headed, though he checks the rearview mirror with a paranoid frequency. Happy's lost in thought, or recollection—something. The lines of her face turn down like the linens of a hotel room bed—a little sad. She closes her eyes. I know how she's feeling. The enervation of the night sinks into my own body. It's in my skin, just below the surface. It takes hold of every part of me. I haven't been this tired in a long time—maybe since October 27th, 2004.

But unlike that night, this morning there's something else. Something riding low beneath the exhaustion. My senses are alive. I'm attuned to the changing colors of the sky—layers of pink and orange like long, flowing brushstrokes across the blue. As the bands of color bend closer to the rising sun, they dilute, like acrylic paint thinned with water, so the color almost disappears into the sunlight. I feel the heat of the bodies in the car around me. And I watch the people in the cars beside me: a man in sunglasses sipping from a travel mug in an SUV, a woman driving with two children in car-seats smiling at a small video in the roof of a van, two teenagers, full of life, singing in a red sports car. I see them at eye level, instead of from above, through glass and cracked blinds. It's different here on the ground. There's possibility here.

Happy sits up and picks Rick's phone up off the back seat without a word. She calls the store, I know because Happy asks about Angel's grandmother. This close to Christmas, he's picked up extra shifts. She asks for her father, provides a brief version of what is about to arrive on his doorstep. She asks him not to freak out, promises to explain everything, then tells him we'll be there soon. She hangs up. In order for Happy to make all of this right, she'll have to expose herself.

I crane my neck to look back at her. "Are you okay?"

She laughs. "I might be."

"Good."

She reaches out with her free arm and squeezes my shoulder once more. "I think so."

"So what the hell happened?" Rick glances in the rearview mirror.

Happy sighs, reaching up and wrapping a hand around the shoulder of my seat to pull herself closer. "After I left Wes's place, I went to stay with my dad. I didn't want to, but I didn't really have a choice, you know?" She raises her eyebrows.

I want to tell her that I didn't really want her to leave, but I don't. Now's not the time. "Didn't he think you had a place of your own?"

"I told him I quit my nannying job when I took this new job and lost my place to stay. I'd be there just until I found my own apartment." She perks up a little. "I've been working full-time at the craft store, and my quilting classes are going well. I figured I could afford to look for an apartment soon."

Rick nods at everything, making it clear he's paying attention, his expression mirroring his absorption in the story. I'm unsure how to react. It's strange to hear this summary of her life. Should I be happy for her? Should I be glad to hear how she's moved on?

"How'd you end up back there?" Rick asks, giving his head a nod in the direction we've just come from.

Happy bites her lip. "I got a call from one of the girls I used to work with. Alma. She asked if we could talk. We met for coffee."

"Was she one of the illegal ones?" I ask. Rick shoots me a hardened look. He's missing context.

"She'd crossed the border from Mexico and had been sending money home to her family. She told me everything. About the prostitution, selling drugs to clients, how Ray had been threatening to call immigration if she backed out. He had a couple other girls participating too. One of them was a runaway. Alma thought she was only fifteen. She was scared just to talk to me but she couldn't take it anymore. Her family was counting on her and she wanted to bring her son here. I told her to clear out, gave her enough money for bus fare. She didn't want anyone else to get in trouble. I told her I'd take care of it, that I wouldn't let anything bad happen to the others."

I turn around, face her. "Why'd you go by yourself?"

"Because I was angry." She shrugs. "And disgusted with myself. I needed to see it."

"But you could have called the police. You could have told your dad." I don't mean to lash out at her. But she needs to be more careful. She could have died tonight. We both could have.

"Wesley." Rick shakes his head.

She crosses her arms. "So, dad, I just wanted you to know

that I've been working in a gentlemen's club for the past year as an adult entertainer and now my old boss and abusive ex-boyfriend are running an illegal brothel out of the basement. We should do something about that, okay?" She pushes the back of my seat. "What do you think?"

I try to imagine having a similar conversation with my father. I think about that first time over five years ago, when he and my mother came to coax me out of the apartment, and I had to turn them away. He tried to manhandle me out the door and I ended up pressed against the cabinets in the corner of the kitchen with my head between my knees, trying to fight off the feeling that my heart was on the verge of igniting. I understand. I give her a nod.

"So I went around closing at 2:00. I'd intended to talk to Ray, but Lee was the only one there. Ray leaves him in charge sometimes." She leans back and settles against her seat. "I demanded to see the rooms. He was worse than I've ever seen him. I should have never gone down there alone."

"You were upset," Rick says entirely without judgment. This is what a good listener does. I try to relax the critical muscles in my own face in imitation.

"When I got down there, I lost my shit. I told him I knew everything and it was over and I was calling the cops. I told him he'd rot in jail, exactly what he deserved. He freaked out and grabbed me." She crosses her arms and shifts against the seat. "I started to get scared. I begged him to let go." She pauses, takes a slow, deep breath. "For a second, I thought he was going to. His grip slackened and I tried to wriggle free. But he got spooked. We struggled and before I knew what was happening, he shoved me up against the wall and I hit the back of my head." She reaches up and massages the back of her scalp. "Everything went black."

"That fucker." Rick's grip tightens on the steering wheel. I agree but I'm too busy watching the tears shimmer at the corners of Happy's eyes to say anything.

"I woke up alone in the basement and climbed the stairs but the door was locked. I tried yelling but no one was in the building. That's when I called Wes."

They both look at me like I'm the strangest part of this whole story.

Their gaze makes me self-conscious. "I guess it's over now." I don't know what else to say. Rick nods in agreement and Happy gives a heavy sigh. So we've reached a consensus. I turn and face forward, lean back against my seat.

Rick turns on the radio. He taps his fingers along to a commercial free hour of holiday tunes—some radio station has the audacity to play twenty-four hours of Christmas music for the entire month of December. It's almost offensive, his selection of holiday cheer, in spite of everything that's happened. But I keep my mouth shut. His eyes are like quarters, shining and round. Is he in shock? It doesn't matter. He's a man of action. He'll drive—do what he has to. He leaves the thinking for after the job is done. In life, I often fault him for this approach. Perhaps, I shouldn't. I'd give anything to be out of my head right now.

When we arrive at the store, we pull around to the back by the loading dock. Mr. Lafferty waits for us, pacing.

"Ready?" Rick asks, looking from the short, stout figure in a tan suit jacket to Happy in the backseat.

She shakes her head. "No."

This isn't how I imagined meeting Happy's father. We pile out of the car and take the small flight of stairs to the back entrance. She reaches out and hugs him.

"Harriet, what in God's name is this?" He tries to sound angry, but his eyes betray his concern.

Happy pulls her arm away. "It's a long story." She motions to the door. "Let's go inside."

Rick nods, averting his eyes from the father figure who stands several inches below him. I'm about to follow but she reaches out and takes my hand.

She smiles. "Dad, I want you to meet Wesley Yorstead."

The muscles in his face constrict and his eyes bulge. He's forgotten, for a moment, that he's perplexed and angry at his daughter's obvious predicament. That's the effect of a phantom. People always wish to catch a glimpse, but never expect to really see. It's a shock to the system meeting me like this. "Wesley," he reaches out a hand.

"Nice to meet you." I'm slow to take his hand, hoping he hasn't just come from the butcher block. Though, with everything I've been exposed to this morning, a little raw meat probably wouldn't even make a difference.

He laughs an uncomfortable chuckle. "What brings you out this morning?"

Happy jumps in. "He came and got me." She squeezes my hand. "It's complicated but we're sort of dating."

"We are?" How nice of her to let me know.

Mr. Lafferty looks at Happy and then up at me and his face scrunches. He cocks his head to the side and his staring makes me squirm. He takes a quick breath and exhales a heavy stream of air out through his nose. Then, his lips curl into a faint smile. "I thought you'd be shorter."

Chapter 6

Happy and I sit in his small back office. The space is cramped and cluttered. A half- empty coffee mug rests on a yellow fast food napkin. Framed photographs cover the wall— pictures of the store in various stages of development. Some show community events. Others show Mr. Lafferty—his arm around the shoulders of an eclectic array of employees. Everyone looks happy—so many smiles. On the desk is a silver picture frame with a posed photo of a much younger Mr. Lafferty and his wife. She's seated. He stands with a hand on her shoulder before a blue-gray background. She has the same instinctive smile as Happy. An attractive wood frame holds a photo of Happy, a blurry close up of the Arc de Triomphe in the background. He keeps the most important people in his line of sight at all times.

William Lafferty is unlike my father in a number of ways. When my father would be abrasive and domineering, Mr. Lafferty is jovial and patient. He listens to Happy's story with only a few interruptions, and then censures himself and goes back to listening. He's disappointed but, in the end, he's proud that his daughter took a stand. It's clear by the end of their interaction that father loves daughter, and daughter cares a great deal about what father thinks. It's so natural, so unconditional, that I have to excuse myself. This is a private moment I shouldn't witness. I've never known families like this. I should find Rick anyway.

It's strange to see the store exist here, in the space of an entire room, when I'm used to thinking of it as only that which fits inside my grocery bags. There's a deli with shaved meats and cheeses, along with prepared meals and sandwiches. A young woman nods from behind the case, a net pulling back her straw colored hair. The butcher block has a small but upmarket selection of meats and seafood. A man in a white butcher coat stained with blood stands ready to help. Across from this area, toward the center, is a large bin of frozen foods. To the far left is a produce section with fresh fruits and vegetables more vibrant than a Cezanne still life. Large shelves of dry goods of every variety stock the central aisles, along with a small bakery case filled with decadent desserts and fresh baked breads. A refrigerated shelf with dairy and cold beverages takes up the far right wall. There's something comforting in the organization of it all. What could I find wandering through the store? It's different calling with a list. I've forgotten what it's like to discover something I wouldn't have thought to request.

I head back into the employee area. The break-room has a vending machine, a few small tables, and a couch. Along one wall is a counter with a sink, a toaster, a microwave and coffee maker. In the corner by the fireplace stands a Christmas tree — about six feet tall — decorated with a hodgepodge of ornaments. Some look handmade and childish. I wonder if they're from Happy's school days. The gold star on top of the tree sits twisted—crooked against the low ceiling of the room. It doesn't fit. Rick's sitting at a table.

He looks up and he sees me in the entrance. "Hey."

"Hey." I sit down on the edge of the couch, careful to avoid the spot in the middle. It's covered in crumbs. We sit in silence until Happy finds us.

"How'd it go?" Rick asks her, his voice full of concern.

She smiles. "As well as can be expected."

I look at her. "Your father loves you."

She sits down beside me on the couch, ignoring the crumbs, and rests her hand on my leg. "He does." She squeezes my thigh. "I still can't believe you're here."

What do I say to this? Thanks? Neither can I? None of these answers do justice. I'll change directions instead. "Where's your father?"

"Waiting for the police." She leans her head back against the cushions and closes her eyes. She's exhausted. Maybe she should come stay with me, rest in the quiet of my apartment.

That's ridiculous. Everything she's said and done, taking my hand, what she said to her father about us, are reactions to what has just transpired. When we go back to my apartment and the danger has subsided, she'll get bored again. I can't ask her to do that.

"That's good." I rub my temples. "Why'd you say we were dating?"

Rick clears his throat, I suppose to remind us he's still here.

Happy doesn't seem to notice. "Knee-jerk response." She takes my hand. "I *have* missed you."

My chest tightens. I don't mind it this time. "You too."

She squeezes. "God, I don't even know what to say. I never thought we'd actually be here, you know?"

"In trouble?"

She cocks her head. "In my dad's store."

"Oh." That makes sense.

"Anywhere." She shifts so she's facing me on the couch. "I can't believe you did this. For me."

Rick gets up and moves for the exit without a word.

"It wasn't just for you." I'm starting to understand that now. "I did it for me, too."

"Thank you." She sniffs and her tired eyes are glossy again. "On both accounts."

She seems so small to me right now, the bones jutting out from her shoulders. Perhaps for the first time I see her for what she is. She is a girl, a woman, full of love and life but weighted down by all the times that passion has led her down a narrow road with the wrong kind of guide. She's a fighter—no doubt. She pulls herself through, even when the tangled memories wrap themselves around her ankles. Every day, she has to break free again and run. This is too much. I don't want to be the one responsible for breaking her this time. Besides, her gratitude only drives home what I've just done, what could have happened in that small room, the place we left them standing. My insides tighten. I can't.

"Where's the bathroom?"

She exhales. Releases my hand. Smart. "Down the hall, to the right," she says.

I get up, stretch, then move out into the hall and find the door marked *Men*. I make sure to lock it.

This whole morning, the emotion—it's too much. I just want to go home. I want to go back to my drafting table and pick up my pen and sketch imaginary figures with imaginary feelings. You put it down on paper and then walk away, wash the ink from your hands. If something doesn't work, you tear it up, start over. Life is harder to erase. Once you lay down a few lines, it's permanent. The tracks always move forward, no matter where they're headed.

I turn on the faucet and splash some water on my face. People always do this in movies. I'm not sure it helps. The chill of the liquid against my skin gives me a momentary jolt, but then I am just cold and wet, confused about why I did it in the first place. I grab a few paper towels and blot my face. Then, I pull the lid down and sit on the toilet seat. I try to breathe deep. I imagine that this is my bathroom—clean and organized—not a public facility. I'm sitting on my toilet, having just turned on the faucet at my sink. I picture the layout. The cabinet and the drawers—how everything fits.

Then I visualize Happy's curling iron with the electric blue cord. Each morning, I'd put it back in the drawer, only to find it out again the next time she used it. I see Happy's purple toothbrush in the holder next to mine, her cinnamon flavored toothpaste in wasteful globs on the side of the sink. My apartment is not my apartment anymore. At least, it is not the same place it was before. It can't be. I won't let it. The space has changed—or I have. The point is, it's different now. Everything is different.

I'm outside this morning for the first time in five years because I chose to be. I chose to —

Happy screams. I hear muffled voices. The air crackles against the surface of my skin. I check to make sure the door's locked. I'm safe. Here, alone in this bathroom, I'm protected from whatever's out there. Out there with everyone else. I should feel relieved. But all I can think about is her scream. It echoes in my head.

I have to go.

I open the door an inch at a time, careful not to let it creak. Then, I step out into the hall. I can hear the voices amplify as I edge closer to the break-room. People argue. Happy tries to reason but a fierce voice tells her to shut up, and then I hear a forceful crack as a hand makes contact with bare skin. It's Lee. I thought this was over. I should go out to the loading dock and wait for the police. They'll be here any minute. I can prepare them. But I've tried waiting for help to arrive before. What if something happens while I'm standing outside with my hands in my pockets? I can't let that happen.

I peer into the doorway.

"I tried to let you go." Lee stands in the middle of the room, rocking back and forth on his feet. His cheeks are wet with tears and his nose runs. His eyes are bloodshot and narrow. He has both hands pressed to his head. In his right hand, he's holding a gun. My stomach plummets and my knees almost buckle. He scratches his head with the butt. "You've ruined everything," he spits. He's even more jerky than that night in my apartment. What is he on? Maybe if I can get behind him, I can take him by surprise. Somehow. I side step into the room, my back to the wall, and take a few steps.

Happy and Rick stand in front of Lee. Rick has his hand on Happy's shoulder. She cowers, holding the side of her face. Lines of tears streak her cheeks. Her father is on the couch. He looks like he's been hit over the head. His scalp bleeds, the blood running down the back of his neck and pooling against his tan jacket collar. His eyes are closed. No one seems to notice me. I take a few more steps along the wall. What will I do when I get behind him?

"Now, you've brought *them* into this." He motions around the room with the gun, first at Rick and then at Mr. Lafferty. Then, he catches sight of me against the wall. My stomach does a nose-dive as his eyes widen. "You," he says with a wave of his gun. "Get the fuck in here." He nods in the direction of Happy and Rick. I take a few unsteady steps and come to stand on the other side of Happy. I take her hand and he points the gun in our direction. His hand shakes, but his finger is on the trigger. "What do you have to say for yourself?"

I'm going to get shot. I can already feel the warm blood seeping through my clothes. Chest wounds bleed heavily — I've seen it. I've seen the red pool spread across a stark white shirt like someone just lowered a paper towel over spilled juice. It's messy — impossible to stop the bleeding, no matter how hard you try. You can grab for dirty rags used to wipe the counters, but the blood soaks through in a matter of seconds. You can press so hard you feel the indentation of the bullet hole through the cloth, like a hole in a bucket that's sprung a leak. A wound so small, an 8 mm piece of metal, can slow the beating heart of a two hundred pound man until it can't pump any longer. You watch the blood run out of the body until there's nothing left, while you wait for sirens in the distance. And you can hold the husk of a person with blank eyes and nothingness, as the ambulance arrives and you know it's too late.

"Just calm down, Lee." Happy's voice is pleading. "No one has to get hurt."

"No one has to get hurt?" He cried out. "What about me? I was somebody there. Now what? You did this to me. Both of you." Lee holds my gaze and something in the hazy blue of his bloodshot eyes make it impossible to look away. He looks at me like he knows me, like he understands something about me. We're connected by a pale figure with red hair. Then, his shoulders heave with a sigh like helium expanding in a hot air balloon. He looks down at the floor, taps the gun against his head again. "This is all your fault."

He points the gun square at me. Is this how the convenience store clerk felt moments before the young man pulled the trigger? Here I am, standing before the gun, and I feel it in my chest as he must have felt it, as though Lee has actually pulled the trigger. A small spot on the left side, right where my heart is, erupts in pain. At this range, I know he's not going to miss. The agony radiates from there. It streams out across my skin, my muscles, as though someone has reached in and pulls at the flesh, tears my chest open as I stand helpless. I can't breathe. Bands of light streak across my line of sight as my vision sharpens and blurs, goes in and out of focus.

"Am I shot?" I gasp, ready to collapse. "Am I bleeding?"

I reach up and put my hands to the spot where I can feel the warm blood flow.

"What the fuck?" He's looking at me as though I'm the one with the gun. He lowers the weapon just a little, and Rick makes a move. He lunges, grabs hold of Lee's arm, and the gun discharges.

Happy screams again. There's a burning in my right shoulder, as though I've been tipped by a poker that's been left sitting in the fireplace. I stumble backward at the shock of it, bump into the couch. I sit down.

Happy rushes to me. "Oh God, Wes."

I look down. The red blood spreads across my shirt, darkening the fabric. At the sight of it, a swell of panic rises up in me, but it doesn't last. It's as though I've flipped a switch and disconnected from my body.

Rick doesn't let go of Lee. He looks at me, his face ashen, and then erupts as he grips both of Lee's arms tight, tries to wrap them behind his back. Lee drops the gun but doesn't let go of Rick. Happy doesn't watch them. She looks at me. Her movements are feverish. Her limbs tremble. I don't feel her hands press into my shoulder. I don't hear what she says in my ear. Rick and Lee have tangled together as they move across the floor, swinging punches. They knock a table over but the room seems quiet to me. Lee manages to get Rick in a choke hold.

Happy screams, "Stop!"

Rick's face reddens in Lee's grip.

Then, I lose focus. My body takes over. Blood trickles down my chest. Happy's hands are covered. It's a lot of blood. My vision blurs and I blink. Happy shakes me, cups my cheek. So this is what death feels like. I look around the room again. Rick will die. I will die. Happy will die. Happy's father will die. Lee will live and continue to do bad things because that's the way the world works. It was foolish for me to think otherwise—even for a second. Ray's probably on a plane leaving the country by now. I'm about to resign myself to this sad fact, turn myself over to the exhaustion amplified in every part of me, when Lee lets out a cry of pain and collapses to his knees. Rick hobbles out of the path as Lee falls forward, flat on his face—unconscious.

Angel stands where Lee has just been, a baseball bat in hand. "Mr. Yorstead, you came outside."

Now I close my eyes.

The Beginning

Happy and I are sitting on a park bench, just on the other side of the bridge. There's snow on the grass, but the walkways are clear and the cement steams, melting icy patches. A woman walks by with a small, white dog on a flashy pink leash. She nods at us as she passes. There's a jogger across the way. His gray sweats are stained with perspiration. I take a deep breath. We have disposable cups from the coffee place across the street. We walked over there first. Needed something warm to combat this weather. The soy cambric is as good as I remember.

Happy sips her coffee with a gloved hand. Her other hand rests on my thigh. "How's your arm?" she asks. She's talking about the one that's still in a sling—hopefully for only a week longer.

It's funny. For all my worrying about being shot, I never expected it to happen. When it did, it wasn't at all like how I imagined it would be. Perhaps it was adrenaline, or shock, or any of the physiological reactions the body produces to cope with physical trauma, but it was more painful to imagine what it would feel like than to actually feel it. The pain came later—in the hospital bed—after blood transfusions and a fentanyl drip—

nothing but brief flashes. Happy holding my hand. Rick pacing at the foot of my bed. Police officers. I remember my mother sitting in a chair beside my bed, her hand on my forearm. My father arguing with a doctor outside the door.

After the haziness wore off a little, and my shoulder began to ache, a doctor came. I listened as he explained how the bullet hit my clavicle and fragmented. Tiny pieces were stuck inside my bone. The doctor thought it would be more dangerous to try and remove the remaining metal than to just let the bone heal around. My father protested but the doctor won. It would stay inside of me, a memento from the night I'd only started to recall with any clarity. I found out later that the police took Lee into custody while they loaded me into an ambulance along with Happy and her father. They found Ray at home with his wife and children. He was waiting for them. He went willingly. People will never stop surprising me.

"It's fine," I lie. It throbs a little, though not as bad as it used to, and I'm only taking Advil now. I take a sip of my drink. It's been a struggle, getting used to using my left hand for everything. Of course it had to be my drawing arm.

"Good," she says. Then, she leans over and gives my shoulder a soft peck. She's been doing that a lot. I don't mind it.

It will be several weeks before the pain in my arm subsides enough for me to draw. It may never go away—not entirely— but it will lessen. Rick thinks the break is good. He's been finishing our manuscript, working through the edits. I've never seen him so passionate. One night, not long after I came home, he asked me what I thought would happen after the final frame, when Scout stands at Arthur Radley's door, imagining his life for just a moment. I told him I was sure they hadn't seen the last of Boo. He liked that ending. He keeps saying when my arm is better, we should do an original story. For the first time, I'm considering the idea that I might have a story to tell.

"Are you warm enough?"

"I'm fine." Another small fib. Happy thinks it's good for me to get out and move around, even if it's the beginning of February.

After a week in the hospital, I came home. I stood at the threshold of my apartment, my arm in a sling, looking at the closed door from the outside. The peephole had been fixed while I was gone. Happy called it a Christmas miracle. She's been staying with me, helping out around the apartment, sitting with me when the painkillers wear off in the middle of the night. She's been sleeping on the couch. I've had to sleep propped up on pillows in the center of my mattress anyway.

People are constantly visiting. Angel brought me some of his grandma's famous tamales. Happy heated them up and we ate them while we watched a movie. My parents come over once a week. My mother makes dinner. Sometimes Mr. Lafferty comes too. We all eat together. I haven't kicked anyone out again. It seems once I let myself out into the world again, I made connections to people and situations that didn't stop when I returned home. I guess that's why we're sitting in the park today.

I leave my apartment now—a little. I don't have a choice. Doctors' appointments and court dates. But it's more than that. I've found I can travel to a few places outside of my bedroom, my kitchen, and my couch. When Happy comes with me, even though anything could turn into a problem, at least I don't face it alone. There'll always be hypotheticals. What if Angel hadn't walked in and found the gun? I don't like to think about it. But I was there and Happy was there and we were together and it was enough.

I have no desire to get myself a car. It's even less probable I'll become one of those bike riding, green people. Helmets are not as safe as you think. I have no long-term plans to travel. Going through the picture albums of Happy's year in Europe is grueling enough. But, I've also started visiting Dr. Kidman the way the average neurotic does—in his office. Turns out I was wrong about Dali and O'Keefe—he's a Rothko square. But he accepts my artistic criticism. He visited when I came home from the hospital and told me he was sorry for the things he didn't say. I told him none of that mattered now. He's happy to have me in his office. Gas is expensive and I'm saving him a lot of miles. He likes to see me there too.

"We need to talk," Happy says with a wry grin.

"I know."

"We can take it slow, you know?" She squeezes my leg. "As slow as you need it to be."

If I could, I'd put my arm around her now. I don't want to take it slow. We've already found each other in new ways. I want to continue to explore. I want to know the parts of Happy I haven't yet, the parts that would mean I'd have to let go of myself in the process. I'm ready for that now, to be with her in every way. For the first time I can remember, my desire is stronger than my fear.

"I'm tired of slow," I say. Then, I lean over and press my lips to hers. This February day isn't as cold as I thought.

She breaks away. "Good." Her look says it's time to go back to the warmth of my apartment.

I give her a nod. "Okay."

Happy stands and takes my coffee cup so I can push myself off the bench with my working arm and get to my feet. She throws the cups away and then comes back and takes my hand. She leans into me as we walk back across the bridge. I look up at the window on the third floor, the one where I've spent so much time looking out from the inside. It seems so small from down here. I enjoy the view on this side of the glass.

Happy walks just a few steps ahead of me. I like to think this is what she wanted from the beginning, with that first vase of horrible daisies she placed in my kitchen. And I'd like to think she's content. At least for now. She's not moving in again, wants to get a studio in Capitol Hill. We're trying to do things the way other new couples do. I don't know how long she'll stick around before she grows tired of being the lighthouse. But I hope there's a chance that won't happen. There's no way to predict where any of this will go. But for now, at least, Happy has pushed me to remember that life bursts with the frantic momentum of Composition 7 and sometimes it's acceptable to let it move.

Acknowledgments

I would like to thank my agent, Susan Ginsburg, for making this an infinitely better book and then working tirelessly to introduce it to the world. I'd also like to thank the wonderful team at Writing Brave Press and Brilliance Audio for giving Wesley a chance.

I owe a great debt of gratitude to the MFA in Creative Writing program at Fairfield University. Not only did the program provide me with the opportunity to write this novel, but it also introduced me to a lifelong creative community and so many wonderful colleagues. I would especially like to thank the following individuals:

Michael Bayer, A.J. O'Connell, and Dan Hajducky, my favorite workshoppers. Eugenia Kim and Rachel Basch for their support and wisdom throughout this process, Allison Kirk— queen of rousing pep talks and brainstorming sessions, Devon Bohm for her brilliance and her willingness to work through the most difficult revisions, Nalini Jones for her indispensable help and guidance throughout many drafts, Thomas Hahn for his profound insights and unwavering friendship, and Scott Schilling for his constant faith and vision for this book and its author—you were right about (mostly) everything.

I'm also blessed with many enduring friendships with lovely people who encourage and sustain me. I'd especially like to thank Rachael and Dan, Lauren and TJ, Kyle, Jaclyn, Raevyn, Katie, and Allison, and Uncle Larry. I'd also like to thank my wonderful community at Abiding Hope Church, who have supported me in so many ways. Thanks Glenn, Doug, Cathi, Laura, Jay and so many others. Finally, so much gratitude to my parents, John and Anne, and my sister, Stacy, for their love and support, and to Hope, Faith, and Dakota for bringing so much joy into my life. I am blessed in so many ways to have such an amazing family and I couldn't do any of this without them. Love to you all.

—Stephanie Harper

About the Author

Stephanie Harper is the author of the award winning fiction novel *Wesley Yorstead Goes Outside,* as well as a poetry collection entitled *Sermon Series*. She received her MFA in Creative Writing from Fairfield University. She's written personal essays and articles for many publications online and in print. She specializes in writing about chronic illness and spirituality. She currently lives in Littleton, Colorado.